I0713151

COSCOM
ENTERTAINMENT

ALSO BY A.P. FUCHS

BLOOD OF MY WORLD TRILOGY

DISCOVERY OF DEATH
MEMORIES OF DEATH
LIFE OF DEATH

UNDEAD WORLD TRILOGY

BLOOD OF THE DEAD
POSSESSION OF THE DEAD
REDEMPTION OF THE DEAD

THE AXIOM-MAN™ SAGA
(LISTED IN READING ORDER)

AXIOM-MAN
EPISODE NO. 0: FIRST NIGHT OUT
DOORWAY OF DARKNESS
EPISODE NO. 1: THE DEAD LAND
CITY OF RUIN
EPISODE NO. 2: UNDERGROUND CRUSADE
OUTLAW
OF MAGIC AND MEN (COMIC BOOK)

MECH APOCALYPSE

MECH APOCALYPSE

OTHER FICTION

A STRANGER DEAD
A RED DARK NIGHT
APRIL (WRITING AS PETER FOX)
MAGIC MAN (DELUXE CHAPBOOK)

THE WAY OF THE FOG (THE ARK OF LIGHT VOL. 1)
DEVIL'S PLAYGROUND (WRITTEN WITH KEITH GOUVEIA)
ON HELL'S WINGS (WRITTEN WITH KEITH GOUVEIA)
ZOMBIE FIGHT NIGHT: BATTLES OF THE DEAD
MAGIC MAN PLUS 15 TALES OF TERROR
UNDENIABLE

ANTHOLOGIES (AS EDITOR)

DEAD SCIENCE
ELEMENTS OF THE FANTASTIC
VICIOUS VERSES AND REANIMATED RHYMES: ZANY ZOMBIE
POETRY FOR THE UNDEAD HEAD
METAHUMANS VS THE UNDEAD
BIGFOOT TERROR TALES VOL. 1 (WITH ERIC S. BROWN)
BIGFOOT TERROR TALES VOL. 2 (WITH ERIC S. BROWN)
METAHUMANS VS WEREWOLVES

NON-FICTION

BOOK MARKETING FOR THE
FINANCIALLY-CHALLENGED AUTHOR
CANADIAN SCRIBBLER: COLLECTED LETTERS OF AN
UNDERGROUND WRITER
LOOK, UP ON THE SCREEN! THE BIG BOOK OF
SUPERHERO MOVIE REVIEWS
GETTING DOWN AND DIGITAL: HOW TO SELF-PUBLISH
YOUR BOOK

POETRY

THE HAND I'VE BEEN DEALT
HAUNTED MELODIES AND OTHER DARK POEMS
STILL ABOUT A GIRL

GO TO
WWW.CANISTERX.COM

MECHAPOCALYPSE

AP FUCHS

COSCOM ENTERTAINMENT
WINNIPEG

For Brian Tanner.

Few guys let me talk time travel as much as I talk about it
with you.

You're a good friend.

MECHAPOCALYPSE

Prologue

THE MISSILE HIT the ground just to the side of the Gambit's hull, rocking Riley Connor in the cockpit. Standing three stories tall, the Gambit was more than equipped to take the shockwave of something going off beside it.

Dust circled around the mech's hull, and Riley switched the scanner off so he could see past it and through the LCD readout screen in front of him. Below, debris littered the city streets: large chunks of concrete and shattered glass from damaged buildings, knocked-over light posts, and dozens of hover-vehicles up in flames. It had to be today the Axiom prototype had to malfunction, trapping its pilot within.

The Axiom had been built as a step up from the Gambit, a mech that was the same in height and width, but one that was lighter and more agile than its predecessor. Originally, the designers wanted to call it the Gambit 2, but later changed their minds, wanting to launch a new line of mech defense in the war against the Supremechs, and saw the potential in a much more maneuverable mech-bot

"Okay, where are you, you sly little—" Riley said to himself, scanning the surrounding area. Up ahead, he caught the tail end of the Axiom rounding the parkade at the end of the street. "There."

He got the Gambit moving, its giant legs quickly gaining ground and getting him to the end of the street in no time. He rounded the corner, the Axiom now in his sights.

With the flick of a switch, he aligned the scope and got the rear of the Axiom's head in view. Inside, behind the pilot's seat, was an array of critical circuits—an emergency kill switch. The problem was the pilot within hadn't activated it so either he didn't know it was there—which was unlikely as that bit of information would've been revealed to him in the briefing before taking it out—or it got damaged and couldn't be activated.

The Axiom rotated its torso and raised its right cannon, a giant blaster on its arm. It blew up a white hover-vehicle that was parked on the street, sending the vehicle up in a brilliant ball of flame and metallic debris.

I hope no one was in there, Riley thought. He raked his fingers through his short brown hair then wiped the sweat off his brow. He checked the scope, zoomed in, and readied what he dubbed the "half-dozen," which were six oval-shaped projectiles that rose out of the Gambit's shoulders like a half-carton of eggs. He counted off slowly, "One, two, three," and sent off a shot to the rear of the Axiom's head. The Axiom turned just as the projectile flew past.

"Great," he said, and watched as the projectile blew out a window in the building across from the Axiom. "Got to be more careful."

He took the Gambit down the street, marveling at the few civilians who lingered around the battleground below as if they didn't have anything better to do.

"Don't get caught in the crossfire," he muttered.

The Axiom dropped its left arm low and, using its flamethrower, laid waste to the first-floor coffee shop of an office building.

Why HQ decided to test this thing so close to the city, he'd never know. He realized they wanted to verify its nimbleness in city streets, but not on the first test. He thought they would've known better. Now, the thing was loose in the city itself and wreaking destruction.

The Axiom squatted down then jumped up, igniting its thrusters and taking off for the sky.

Must be running on autopilot, he thought. *And destruct mode.* "All right, here we go." Riley activated the Gambit's rockets and a moment later he was airborne. From the ground, watching the humanoid-shaped mech with sharp corners rush into the sky was an awesome sight. He should know because even after all these years piloting them, he still got a thrill seeing one take off.

Soaring through the air, Riley adjusted the scanner and quickly located the Axiom some two hundred and fifty meters ahead.

Have to coax it down first, he thought. *Can't knock it out of the sky. Not from this height.*

He pushed a few buttons then switched on the boosters. Immediately, the Gambit shot forward, picking up speed. When he came up alongside the Axiom, he peered at the topaz-colored poly-glass of the head unit, hoping to catch a glimpse of the pilot within. The glass was two-way; he couldn't see through it.

He fired off a chain of bullets across the Axiom's hull, hoping to catch its attention. Its head unit turned to look at him and the mech fired back with its flamethrower. The Gambit took the assault no problem.

Riley returned fire with another scatter of bullets and topped it off with another shot from the half-dozen, targeting the mech's shoulder. The Axiom changed course and started toward him.

"Good, follow me," he said. He turned tail and started to descend, flying just fast enough to keep ahead of the Axiom, but nothing farther. He needed it to follow him.

The two mechs flew lower through the air. The Axiom sent out another wave of flame. Riley veered the Gambit to the side, and from his cockpit window watched the stream of fire streak past. Another rush of flame came in from the other side. Riley banked in the opposite direction and another display of yellow and orange streaked past him.

He rotated the half-dozen on the Gambit's shoulder so it was facing the rear and blasted off one of the lethal projectiles. This one struck the Axiom square in the chest.

If it is on autopilot, he thought, *then it should automatically lock onto me and not rest until I'm taken out.*

The autopilot feature was a lifesaver and had saved many pilots lives during the war. With the autopilot engaged, the mech could keep on fighting if the pilot was unconscious, injured or even dead. However, nothing beat good old-fashioned human instinct in battle hence why the feature wasn't always employed. And some units could even be operated remotely. Unfortunately, right now, the Axiom wasn't one of them; any control from command was not in service.

They were nearing ground level. Riley quickly dropped low and slammed on the brakes. He lurched forward against his safety belt even with the inertia dampeners on. The Axiom flew past overhead.

"Lock on," he told himself and got the rear of the Axiom's head unit in view. Going by the schematic overlay on his screen, he put the kill switch in his sights. The Axiom was some fifty feet ahead. Any moment now it'd turn and seek him out.

Riley fired.

The projectile flew through the air and hit the Axiom square in the back of the head. A small explosion went off and a second later the mech dropped from the sky like a stone. It slammed into the ground full force.

Riley hoped its pilot was okay. At least now the MRUs—Mobile Response Units—could come in and take the situation from here.

The real question was why the Axiom malfunctioned. He wasn't an engineer, only a pilot, but he also knew enough mech history to know that malfunctions of this magnitude rarely happened.

He wondered if something else was going on.

1

FOUR MEN WERE on their knees in front of the Exo-gauntlet, an old exoskeleton that, while not completely obsolete, still had some firepower. Each man had their hands behind their bowed heads, the bruises and spots of blood on their faces evidence they had put up a fight.

The Exo-gauntlet had its cannons pointed at the men's heads. All it'd take would be for one, or even two of them, to try and make a break for it and it'd all be over.

Riley had been called in to deal with whoever was manning the Exo-gauntlet, his men waiting outside the base. He had gone in alone, thinking there was no point in risking the lives of anyone else. It was clearly a robbery gone bad, what with the authorities alerted to the bunker beneath Stake 47, a military base just outside of Winnipeg. No longer active since the Rebirth two years ago, Stake 47 had been the hub of authority and law during the war with the Supremechs, with men and women both on the ground, walking the city streets, to those like Riley who were regulars on the Exo-beat and patrolled in twelve-foot tall exo-suits. Now their base was in the city, Stake 48.

Riley eyed the Exo-gauntlet's hulking gray and green form through Visor-7, hardware on the suit itself but software for the user interface. The readouts on the Exo-gauntlet didn't raise alarm. It was the hostages that were the worry. To try and stealthily go in on foot and take the Exo-gauntlet on would be suicide. Besides, any arms presently at his disposal wouldn't stand a chance. He'd need something that packed more firepower than a mere automatic. Unfortunately, anything bigger wouldn't fit with him inside the exo-suit he was in.

The Renosis-4, which he piloted, stood thirteen feet tall, was about six feet wide at the shoulders, with arm cannons, pincers and armed footwear so the machine could fire if ever knocked on its back.

Commander Tiel's voice came through the comm. unit: "We see 'im as you see 'im. Our team is looking for weaknesses in the armor, so though it's an antique, we might be hard pressed to find one never mind two. The Exo-gauntlet's were built strong and steady even back then."

"Roger that," Riley said. "I've got my eye on him. The problem is he knows he's at a standoff and that someone is in the warehouse, but he doesn't know where I am."

"I'm sure it won't be long until he figures out you're behind that stack of crates off to the side."

"Was thinking of taking an aerial view, hide up in the rafters."

"He'll hear your thrusters if you do that."

"Exactly."

Riley fired up the thrusters mounted to the back of the Renosis-4 and made a show of their light flickering off the wall in behind the storage crates. He then pulled on the throttle inside the arm unit next to the trigger and let the Renosis-4 rise up all the way to the roof before cutting the power.

Immediately the Exo-gauntlet shifted its stance and aimed one cannon up at the rafters, the other remaining on the hostages.

Unless the Exo's night vision was activated, Riley knew he'd be invisible up here in the shadows. He quickly took the Renosis-4 running along the rafter then, once on the other side, fired up the thrusters again, making a show of the lights. The Exo-gauntlet's other cannon left the men and aimed high at his position.

Riley dropped a flare; it landed on the rafter and lit up, sending off a stream of red light and smoke. Again, he flashed the thrusters. When he did, the Exo-gauntlet's cannon fired and a ray of heat came for him. He blasted the thrusters one last time then cut the power and dropped down into the shadows. The heat ray from the Exo-gauntlet's cannon cut through the rafter beam, slicing the metal in two.

Now with the Exo's attention diverted, Riley fired off another flare—this one a crackler—off to the opposite side. The flare ignited and another stream of red light shone forth in wild bursts, mimicking the light pattern of his thrusters. The Exo-gauntlet sent off another heat ray into the corner of the room.

The men on their knees ducked down. Had Riley's Renosis-4 been closer, he might've been able to scan the security tags hanging off the men's uniforms and found out their identities and positions, perhaps gain some clue as to why whoever was manning the Exo-gauntlet was in the bunkers beneath Stake 47. At the same time, he knew the men worked security, guarding Stake 47 from any trespassers.

Riley rounded the far side of the room, sticking to the shadows. Within moments he was parallel to the Exo-gauntlet and, a moment after that, was able to come in behind it.

Off to the side, he fired up his thrusters and made a beeline for his target. The two exo-suits crashed together, tumbling to the side.

On top of the Exo-gauntlet, Riley squeezed his fists together inside the Renosis-4, making the unit do the same. He struck the Exo in the chest, hopefully rattling whoever was inside. Another blow, this one delivered to the head, hopefully sent the message he meant business. What he needed to do was try and fire a light shot to the exo unit and blast it open, reveal whoever was inside.

The Exo-gauntlet raised its cannon and aimed it directly at the Renosis-4's head. A second later, it blasted off a beam of heat. Inside the suit, Riley's skin immediately began to sweat. He could only imagine how hot the outer hull must be and, despite its ability to withstand extreme temperatures, a few more shots like that and he'd have to abandon the suit.

The Exo-gauntlet kicked him off it and sent him flying back. Riley punched on the thrusters again and flew straight at his prey. Another blast of heat sent him veering off to the side.

Come on, you're in something stronger, he thought. *Get it together!* He sent off two shots of his own, these striking the Exo-gauntlet dead on. The Exo-gauntlet backed away.

"Good, you better run," Riley said.

A moment later, the Exo-gauntlet sent off another wave of heat, setting off the Renosis-4's alarm.

"Are you serious?" Riley said. He had hoped to take whoever was in the Exo-gauntlet alive, but if they were going to try and kill him, he knew that might not be the case. Quickly, he fired off another shot and blasted the Exo-gauntlet against the wall. He sent in another, this time ramping up the damage on the controls inside the forearm. Every time he punched at the keys, he reveled in having their placement memorized since they weren't visible to his eyes and were inside the arm.

The Exo-gauntlet stumbled back. Riley shot off another blast. In such tight quarters it struck the Exo hard and sent it tumbling. While it rolled backward, the Exo-gauntlet sent off another heat ray and the interior of the Renosis-4 got unbearably hot. Either the specs on the Exo-gauntlet were off, or some modifications to the weaponry had been made.

Riley spoke into the comm. "Anytime you guys want to feed me some weaknesses, I'm all ears."

"Copy that," Tiel said. "If there are any, we'll let you know, but to be honest, that thing was built solid. You might be on your own."

Figures. Send me in to ensure the hostages live only to have me die in the end. Thanks.

Riley blasted the Exo-gauntlet again. It tumbled back.

Above, the rafter beams began to creak and groan. The sound of bending metal grated on his ears.

"What is that?" he asked.

"We can hear it through your comm. Where's that coming from?"

Riley adjusted his line of sight to the ceiling. The rafter beams were buckling in places. Dust and debris rained down.

A second later, holes punched through the roof.

"You sent in reinforcements," Riley said.

"Wasn't us."

"Oh great."

Three more Exo-gauntlet units punched through the ceiling and rode their thrusters down beside their fallen comrade. Once they touched down, they had their weapons trained on Riley.

"What should be your last words before you die?" he asked himself. *Please don't let that question be the last thing I say.* "Run."

He pivoted the Renosis-4 around just as the other Exo-gauntlets sent off a stream of heat rays at him. He barreled in between the storage crates. Several went up in flames behind him.

"Keep going!" he shouted into his comm. Why into the comm. unit, he didn't know. Maybe it was so those on the other end could hear just how much trouble he was in.

Explosions went up behind him. He fired up his thrusters and made for the elevator shaft he had taken down, back when he was first sent in.

"Good luck trying to sift through this once things cool down," he said as he ascended up the shaft and into the base proper. He checked his sensors to see if anyone was following him.

For the time being, the coast was clear.

But that also meant whoever was piloting the Exo-gauntlets got away and those poor men were likely dead.

And it had been his fault.

2

THE NEXT DAY, Riley rode the elevator down to Sublevel 7, hands behind his back, legs shoulder-width apart, and his stance not for formality. He was nervous. Commander Tiel wanted a word with him and he could only guess it was because he'd let whoever was manning the Exo-gauntlet get away. Worse, let all *four* of them get away.

It wasn't your fault, he told himself. *You were surrounded. It was either bolt or join the Graveyard.* Eagle Park Cemetery— or "the Graveyard," as it was called around base—was where those in service who died during the war and through other incidents afterward were buried.

The lights above the elevator door counted down until the 7 lit up in orange. It flickered; the bulb needed fixing.

Riley got off and headed down the hallway in front of him. A couple of guards manned their posts by doors running off the hallway. Once at the end, he turned left, then made a right a few meters later. Tiel's office was past this room and in the back. At the door, Riley steeled his nerves and then knocked.

"Come in," Commander Tiel said. Before Riley could say anything, he added, "Sit down."

Riley took a seat in the metal chair in front of Tiel's desk. To his left was a bank of monitors Tiel used to watch the action on the surface.

Commander Tiel stood behind his desk and held a data pad in his right hand, the other hand on his hip. The man was only forty-two, but looked fifty-five, his hair having already turned all gray three years ago.

War ages a man.

At least Tiel was off the ground for the most part and barked out orders from either his office or the Combat Monitoring Room elsewhere on Sub-level 7.

Tiel wore his standard olive green combat pants and matching shirt. Rarely was he seen wearing anything else.

Riley was curious what the man was looking at on the data pad.

Tiel reached into his breast pocket and pulled out a cigar, the action almost robotic—automated—and put the cigar between his lips. Eyes never leaving the data pad, he pulled a Zippo—an antique lighter—from the same pocket and fired it up. Riley had a thing for Zippos, too, and had three in his collection in his bunker: one silver, one brushed nickel, the other a rare metallic blue. Tiel lit the cigar, puffed a few times to get it going, then put the Zippo back in his pocket. Without saying a word, he turned his back to Riley and focused on the data pad.

Riley debated letting out a sigh or clearing his throat or tapping his thighs to subtly remind his superior he had just called him into his office. Did the man forget he was here? Or was this some tactic to wear him down a little before whatever news Tiel had to share was dropped? Or even a ploy to get him to confess to cowardice, waiting for him to take responsibility for yesterday's failure?

I was trained better, he thought.

Minutes passed and not once did Tiel give indication he was finally going to speak.

Finally, he adjusted his stance, giving Riley hope . . .

. . . then went back to reading.

What was he looking at? Why summon him down here only to stand there and read? Couldn't he have read the information *before* calling him down here?

Commander Tiel took a long puff on his cigar, the smoke curling around his head. He cleared his throat, then turned around.

"Connor," Tiel said. His voice was stern yet carried a strong hint of disappointment. "You're in some hot water. A lot of hot water, actually."

"Look, sir, in my defense—"

"Can it." He shook his head. "Not now."

Oh great, Riley thought.

Tiel continued. "Stake 47 was a secure facility. Unused, but secure. We haven't had so much as a mouse go inside there since decommissioning it. In fact—and this is between you and me—security was still up and running in different parts throughout her."

"Why?"

"I said can it. I'm talking. Not you."

"Sorry."

Tiel shot him a look. Apparently even apologizing wasn't allowed right now. "Understand this: what went on yesterday wasn't someone simply trespassing. They had gotten in using an Exo-gauntlet suit and managed to stay undetected until they hit the storage unit. That's when you went in."

Riley had been wondering how long his superiors knew about the trespasser before they took action. Now he knew.

After taking a puff of his cigar and slowly breathing out the smoke, Tiel said, "We don't know who did it. And what you don't know is that a handful of Exo-gauntlet suits were stolen from this facility four months ago. No word or sign of them since. Whoever stole them had dismantled the trackers. Now we know there was a purpose meant for them."

"Any idea who took them?"

"What did I say about talking?"

"Sorry."

"Using the suits could be how they bypassed some of the security in Stake 47. As you know, each suit has a built-in clearance signal. What these guys didn't know was that Stake 47 had security that ensures no one—and I mean no one—can just waltz in there unannounced. The mystery is how these folks knew Stake 47 was used as a kind of vault for certain items of interest. I suspect an inside job or, at the very least, leaked information. At the same time, that shortens the list of where the leak could've come from because not very many knew all Stake 47 contained." He took a puff of his cigar. "We took inventory after what went down yesterday."

Let me guess—

"Something was missing," Tiel said.

Called it.

"Something important."

Riley wasn't sure if he should speak yet so he held his tongue.

"*You're* in trouble not because you let them getaway—as disappointed in that as I am—but that you didn't ask for backup."

"There was only one exo-suit. It was a fair fight."

"You *thought* there was only one exo-suit. Turned out there were others just waiting to ambush."

"I had no choice but to get out of there. It was either that or become scrap."

"I get that and" —he leaned forward on the desk— "it was the right call. You're trained to get outta Dodge if there's no other choice, but it's this Maverick mentality of being the hero that's gotten you in trouble today."

Should I fight him on this? It was one *on* one. *It was a fair fight.*

"Others were waiting outside. You went in alone. It stops now, do you understand?" Tiel said.

Riley nodded.

"I said, do you understand?" His voice was like steel.

"Yes, sir." There was silence between the two men, so quiet Riley could hear the tobacco burning on Tiel's cigar when he sucked back on it. *Time to play it humble.* Riley took a breath then exhaled slowly. "Can I ask what was stolen, sir?"

"You can ask."

"Um, well, what was stolen?"

"I only said you could ask. Now get out and let me finish writing you up."

"But . . ."

"Get. Out."

♦ ♦ ♦

Riley headed back down the hallway toward the elevator. That little display in Tiel's office didn't make sense; at least, the offence wasn't as serious as Tiel made it out to be.

Then again, the bad guys did get away. You should always go in in pairs. Commander Tiel had been right about that part.

The thing was, when gathered outside Stake 47 yesterday with the other exos, Riley wanted to play the hero.

Now he was paying for it.

Riley spent the night in his bunker, sleeping off and on, trying to read an old paperback he found amongst the ruins of a bookstore a year ago. It was a superhero novel about a guy in a blue cape who flew around his hometown. It wasn't that the book was boring—far from it—but he was so disappointed in himself that it sucked the life out of him, made him sleepy. Was it stories like these that fueled his hero complex? Did he have this thing about putting himself on a pedestal and figuring if something needed to get done only he could do it? Hadn't he proved he was fully capable of getting done what needed doing after his service in the war, or was it just his ego talking?

Laying there, he wished for some company. Maybe Sophie Jones was still up?

3

STEADY THUMPING GREETED Riley's ears when he approached Sophie's door. Something was banging up against it. Something small.

He knocked.

The thumping continued, and just as he was about to knock again, it stopped. A moment later the door was unlatched and he heard clicks as she undid the locks.

The dorms. Those in service at Stake 48 lived there. Some officers resided with their families. Single folks, like himself and Sophie, resided with themselves.

She opened the door. Her long brown hair was pulled back in a ponytail, her bangs hanging around her eyes. Her rugged eggshell sweater and gray khakis hugged her athletic frame and his heart did a little dance like it always did. She held a purple rubber ball in her hand, the source of the thumping.

"Thought you might be up," he said.

"You know me," she said, "I never sleep." She smiled. "What's up?"

"Got a minute?"

"For you, Riley, I got three."

"Funny."

She pulled back into the dorm and let him in. He closed the door. Her place was the same layout as his: about two hundred square feet of living space in rectangle form. Four room dividers were allotted per personnel to partition the room how one wanted. She used three. One for the living room and kitchenette, another for a bedroom, the last for the bathroom.

She went over to the futon across from the door and said, "Do you mind?" She raised her hand with the ball.

"Sorry," Riley said and got out of the way.

Sophie threw the ball against the door. It hit the floor as it bounced back. She caught it, then did it again. "What brings you here?"

"Nothing much. Just bored."

"Oh. Thought you'd want to talk about what happened yesterday."

"Does everybody know?" he asked.

"Only those who matter." She smirked.

He sighed. "Was called into Tiel's office earlier."

"Yeah? How'd that go?"

"About as good as all the other times."

"He mad you botched the operation?"

"I didn't botch it. I just . . . didn't come through."

"Well, for what it's worth, I think you made the right call."

"There was four of them."

"I would've done the same thing."

"Wish Tiel would've done the same thing, too."

She kept bouncing the ball. Riley found it distracting. It wasn't that he was here for advice or even to vent. He'd simply wanted company because he was bored and he could always count on Sophie for a good time. They'd gone to the academy together, hit it off as friends, and was always in each other's corner for when the other needed somebody. As for anything more than that, he tried hinting at it once or twice, but she was the kind of girl that made him feel like he had to be extra careful when around her, the idea that if he told her he had a thing for her, she'd bolt and their friendship would be over. As a friend, though, she was everything anyone could hope for: loyal, a confidante, fun, and had this way when talking to her that she made you feel like you were the only one who mattered.

Even when seemingly distracted by bouncing a ball against the door.

"Did he ream you out?" Sophie asked.

"Just played the strong silent type." Riley stuck his hands in his pockets and began to pace. "What was intriguing was that he said something was stolen."

"Yesterday?"

"Yeah. I asked him what and he wouldn't tell me."

"Think it was important?"

"I think so. At least, important enough not to tell someone in a lower rank like me."

"Any idea what it was?" She caught the ball, held it a few moments and rolled it back and forth between her hands before resuming bouncing it again.

"No. No real way to find out either."

"Does it matter?"

"Considering it was my operation?" He stopped pacing. "It'd be nice."

"You could always press him for it."

"He won't say anything. Not Tiel."

"And he's your commanding officer. Go to anyone else inquiring about it and you'd be sure it'd come back to him."

Riley started pacing again. "Wish he didn't have it out for me."

"He doesn't have it out for you."

"As if."

"As if I'm right," she said with a grin. "The guy knows you're good at what you do. Why do you think he called you in yesterday even though it wasn't your shift?

You man the exos like they're a part of your body. He knew he could count on you to get in there and get the drop on whoever was trespassing."

"I *did* get the drop on them."

"Exactly. It might not have gone as planned, but you did what he called you in to do. He probably thinks he's protecting you by not telling you what was at stake."

"Or he's not allowed to."

"Or he's not allowed to. Maybe if he was, he'd say something."

"Now you got me curious."

"You got *me* curious." She caught the ball, squeezed it. "We could always snoop around his office?" She said it like a question. Was she serious?

He stopped pacing again. "Oh yeah? And then what? Get caught, get suspended, maybe even fired."

"You're right, bad idea." She started bouncing the ball again.

Sophie had a way of putting ideas in his head, planting that little seed that would eventually gnaw at him until he gave in. Was that how *she* got what she wanted? Did she know she did it or was it a habit she wasn't aware of?

He had to ask: "How do we do that?"

"Simple" —she caught the ball— "we go in, I take a look at his computer, maybe get some answers."

"You know that area's under guard."

"Not late at night."

He glanced around her place. "Should I take the bed or the couch?"

◆ ◆ ◆

Around two hundred hours, Riley and Sophie found out, Sub-level 7 was guarded by a lone officer, fully armed. The moment the elevator door opened, they heard his footsteps coming to greet them. In a panic, Sophie pressed the close button and the two made it back to the dorm level undetected.

"What are we going to do?" Riley whispered as they walked back to her dorm. The rest of the dorm level was asleep.

Sophie pressed her lips together, squinted, the donkey clearly rounding the tree. Riley waited. Then she said, "Feel like some whiskey?"

Not long after, Riley was back in the elevator, a box of odds and ends in his hand, Sophie's bouncy ball perched precariously on the corner of the box. It teetered on the edge of the box when the elevator landed at Sub-level 7 and the momentum from the ride pushed up against their feet.

"Man, you stink," Sophie said.

"You didn't have to spill it on me," he said.

"Yes, I did. Now go work your magic."

He sighed, and the door opened. Sophie sidled up against the inside of the elevator, out of sight.

Putting on his best show, Riley stumbled out of the elevator and smacked the side of the box with his palm.

"Oh man . . ." he said loudly, then let out a deep chuckle. He dragged his feet along the ground, making extra noise. A second later, footfalls rose on the air. Heart pounding quickly, hoping it'd all work out; he made his way down the hallway.

The officer appeared. Riley didn't recognize him. If the fellow always worked a late shift of some kind, the two wouldn't know each other anyway.

"What're you doing?" the officer asked.

Riley hung around the elevator door. "Whoa, hey man, what're *you* doing?"

The officer neared him, but didn't draw his weapon. "You're not supposed to be here. What's your name and rank?"

"What? I live here."

The officer came up to him then breathed out heavily, clearly smelling the booze. Riley had taken a single shot, but Sophie thought it'd be funny if she went the extra mile and splashed some on his neck and shirt. "You're loaded." The officer eyed the box. "What d'you got there?"

"Just some memories, some things. Been a good night. Taking them home." Riley went to move past the guard.

The officer caught him by the arm. "Not that way, son. You're on the wrong level."

Riley stood up straight, leaned in close and breathed on the man. "*You're* on the wrong level. I'm on the level. I'm a good man."

"Maybe on other days," the officer said, "but tonight you need to turn around, get back in that elevator, and head up to your dorm. Sleep it off."

"I'm not sleeping. Going to go home and—" He moved past the officer and gave the box a quick shuffle. The ball rolled off the corner. Riley feigned like he suddenly couldn't handle the box on his own so nodded toward the ball that rolled off to the side. "Do you mind?"

The officer shook his head in disgust and turned away from him. Just as he bent over to pick up the ball, Sophie darted out of the elevator, grabbed the security card from the clip on the guard's belt, then snuck past him. The officer turned and straightened, none the wiser. "Here"

—he put the ball on the box and shoved it in the corner so it wouldn't fall out— "now go back in the elevator. I'll help."

Riley yawned and stumbled forward, bumping into the man then leaned up against him. "I'm not sure which way I'm supposed to go. Which way's the elevator?"

"Right behind you."

"Oh." Riley turned and went in then stared at the buttons.

"You need to push them," the officer said.

"My hands are full."

"Or for goodness sake," the man said and got into the elevator with him. "Let's see some ID. I'll take you back."

"Back pocket," Riley said. "Want a drink?"

4

Sophie used the security card and entered Commander Tiel's office. If all went to plan, that poor officer should be in the elevator with Riley now, walking him back to his room. The trade-off was Riley would have to reveal who he was. The payoff was she'd have at least fifteen minutes to snoop through Tiel's files and get out of there.

She logged into Tiel's system. It was password protected. Thankfully, she had an eye for detail and had often watched his fingers trail the keys when she met with him and he was logging in. Though her view had been inverted, she knew what to type. She entered the password. His desktop came up.

While she scanned for recently accessed files, she hoped Riley was fulfilling his end of the plan and stalling the officer as much as possible. He might be a maverick, but he usually kept his nose clean. She knew he was out of his element tonight.

A few files popped up, but nothing showed that would indicate the information she was looking for.

Why was she doing this for Riley? Was it to satisfy his curiosity over what was stolen? Was it her trying to get back at Tiel for not giving her the promotion he hinted at six months ago? Was she trying to prove something to herself?

"Come on," she said as she searched over a few more files. She checked recent communications and messages.

Nothing.

She rolled the chair away from the monitors and, still seated, looked around the office. Her eyes settled on a notepad on Tiel's desk.

Paper.

Only used when an electronic trail was to be avoided. Paper could be destroyed and wouldn't be part of Stake 48's mainframe data backup system.

The paper was blank, but the indents on it . . . . Her eyes widened.

She had been so lost focusing on the piece of paper that the scent of smoke snuck up on her. But she knew that smell.

"Can I help you?" Tiel asked.

◆ ◆ ◆

The officer saw Riley to his room. Once inside, Riley set the box down then said to the guard, being sure to slur his words, "Thank you, Officer, you have a nice evening serving and protecting and all that good stuff."

The comm. unit on the officer's belt came to life. "Lawrence, is there a gentleman smelling of booze with you?"

The officer picked up the comm. unit and brought it to his mouth. "Um, yes, sir."

"Bring him down to my office. He's about to be suspended."

Riley pursed his lips then looked at the box in his arms. So much for stalling. "I guess I should set this down, huh?"

◆ ◆ ◆

Sophie sat in Commander Tiel's chair, a lump in her throat.

Tiel put his comm. unit back on his belt then, with piercing eyes, said, "You are beyond in trouble. Do you have any idea how many rules you're breaking?"

"Just a few?"

"Get up."

She stood and rounded to the other side of the desk. Tiel took his proper place, turned on the desk lamp, then leaned over the desk, both palms planted. "I guess I don't have to pry to find out whose idea this was, do I?"

She cast her eyes down to her hands. *Should I say anything? Probably best to keep my mouth shut.*

"Entering a superior officer's office without permission is a major faux pas never mind doing it after hours when they're not here."

"I'm sorry, sir."

"Sorry won't cut it. When Riley gets down here, you and him have a lot of explaining to do. After that . . . I haven't decided, but it won't be pretty."

She simply nodded quietly.

The minutes ticked by. Tiel eyed her the whole time, clearly playing the intimidation game.

It was working.

Her heart raced and she started running through mental scenarios of either being quarantined in her dorm or being escorted off-base altogether. If she was told to leave, she hadn't any place to go on the outside.

Finally, Lawrence brought Riley to the office door. Riley looked at her and it was clear by the confounded expression on his face that he didn't know how to react. She felt terrible as this whole thing had been her idea.

"Give the man his security card back," Tiel told Sophie.

She sighed, then produced the card and leaned back over the chair to hand it to the officer. Lawrence took it, a surprised look on his face.

"Sorry," Sophie told him.

To Lawrence, Tiel said, "Leave us."

The officer saluted then left.

Tiel finally stopped leaning on his desk, stood straight, and crossed his arms. "You have two minutes."

Riley looked to Sophie. She didn't know what to say.

Riley cupped both hands by his mouth, took a breath, then rubbed his face before saying, "It's my fault. I was upset over what happened and was worried you'd take disciplinary action. I got scared and talked Sophie into coming down here. Thought maybe she could find out what my fate was."

"Your fate?" Tiel said. "You've pretty much sealed it, haven't you?"

"I guess so. I'm sorry, sir," Riley said.

"Sorry won't help. You've violated my privacy, broke and entered—" To Sophie: "You have something to say?"

"Um, was going to say nothing was broke, but never mind."

"You're right 'never mind.' Both of you are confined to quarters until further notice. Don't be surprised if you find yourselves out in the city real soon and *not* to be on duty."

"Yes, sir," Riley said. "Let's go, Sophie."

She stood and headed toward the door. He had covered for her, tried to protect her. As grateful as she was, it didn't feel right. Riley was already out the door when she stopped at it. "Sir?"

"Get out, Sophie."

She swallowed the lump in her throat. "What was stolen from Stake 47?"

"How'd you—Connor, get back in here!"

Riley turned and shot her a hard look. "Way to go."

She shrugged and whispered, "Sorry."

When Riley entered, Tiel said, "What happened to superior-to-officer confidentiality?"

"Well, if you must know" —he ran his hands through his hair— "I've had a lot to drink and—"

"Yet you're talking just fine for the amount of stink on you." If Tiel was anything, he was perceptive. "I'll give you guys points for pulling a fast one. So that's what this is really about? What was stolen at Stake 47?"

Now who's violating superior-to-officer confidentiality? Sophie thought.

"Okay, I'll cut the crap," Riley said. "I want to know what went down. Obviously the operation was important. I ruined it. I get that. I also know you can't tell me unless you're willing to take a chance. I also realize that I'm nobody special and maybe there's no reason for me to know. However, since I was there, don't I have a right to know?"

Tiel seemed to take in his words, but said, "No."

"I'm curious, too," Sophie said, the words coming out before she thought better of it. More so, she was curious if—

"That's nice," Tiel said. To Riley: "I'm under orders to keep this under wraps. It's highly sensitive and highly classified."

"So I guess the answer's no?" Riley said then seemed regretful he had said it after he did.

Way to shut him down, Riley, Sophie thought.

"The answer's no," Tiel said. "Go to your quarters. Both of you."

The two turned and started to leave. Once more Riley was out the door before she was. When she reached the doorframe, she turned and said, "I know about the particle accelerator."

5

COMMANDER WAYNE TIEL was clearly not impressed and he made sure both Riley and Sophie knew it. Yet instead of outright denying what Sophie said, he gave himself away by letting out a defeated sigh when she said the words.

"No point trying to cover up," Riley said. He hoped he was playing this right. News of the particle accelerator was fresh to him.

"You're a smart girl," Tiel said.

"One of the best," she said.

"Don't get cocky. Close the door."

Riley did and he and Sophie got closer to Tiel's desk.

"You realize I don't have to tell you anything," Tiel said.

The two nodded.

Silence hung on the air.

Should I say something? Riley wondered.

Sophie tapped the blank notepad on Tiel's desk. "Says here, 'particle accelerator.'"

Tiel looked at the blank piece of paper. "Says nothing."

"I see the indents in the paper."

"Well played."

"It's not a game," Sophie said, "but it seems you're playing one."

"Watch yourself."

"Sorry, sir, but now that we know, is there anything you can tell us?"

"Nothing I'm authorized to say."

"Look," Riley said, getting his commander's attention, "both Sophie and I clearly want to know what's going on. She found out what went missing. I realize your hands are tied in certain respects to this, but no one needs to know we met tonight."

"Lawrence knows," Tiel said.

"All he knows is Sophie and I got busted for coming in here. He doesn't know anything else. We'll play along with whatever you come up with, but as for the particle accelerator, I'd like to know what it is and why its sudden absence is so top secret."

"You're not going to let this go, are you?" Tiel said.

"No, sir. I can't. It went missing as a result of the operation I was a part of. I feel like I have a hand in this."

"And now I do, too," Sophie said.

Tiel ran his hand through his hair, pulled a cigar out of his pocket, and lit up. "What I'm about to tell you is highly classified. I won't disclose all, let's be clear, but Stake 47 was decommissioned, yes, but partly kept on-line to house items of importance and keep them off-base lest they fall into enemy hands. The particle accelerator was one of those items."

"What does it do?" Riley asked.

Tiel sighed. "Pretty much what its name implies: accelerates particles at the molecular level. It was meant as a component of experimental weapons technology, to be able to bend Time and Space around an object of choice. Think of the possibilities: to be able to launch all our attacks from within the safety of our base with pinpoint accuracy. Imagine firing off a shot here, but be able to program whatever you sent through the wormhole to appear wherever you'd like. We could take out the heads of enemy camps undetected. We could bring down their mech-bots without having to send any of our own out on the field. We could even potentially send a man through for covert operations. Plenty of uses."

"Was it ever tested?" Sophie asked.

"It was, and results were favorable . . . but also unstable. From what I understand, Time and Space is always in motion and one can't always control it."

"You'd almost think the benefits would outweigh the risks," Riley said.

"You would think," Tiel said, "but the technology was nowhere near complete. It was still entry level to the grand plan. You have to build small before you can build big."

Sophie furrowed her brow. "I understand what it was meant to do so realize why it having gone missing is important, but if it's not fully operational or just operational on a small level, why the big secrecy?"

"Because our fear is that whoever took it is building something and needed this component to complete their task. Worse, whoever stole it is either working both sides or knows someone who is." To Riley: "Look at me."

Tiel eyed him coolly, studied him. Riley felt the hairs on the back of his neck stand on edge. *Does he think it's me?*

"You letting the thief go raises suspicion," Tiel said, as if reading his thoughts.

Riley put up his hands. "Don't look at me. I just found out about this now. I had no idea what was at Stake 47. I thought it was shut down and at most had a few things in it that no one was using anymore, like old tables or something."

Tiel still eyed him.

"Look, Riley's innocent," Sophie said.

"And what about you?" Tiel said.

"What about me? I had no idea about any of this until Riley came crying to me earlier and—"

"I wasn't crying."

"Sorry, *complained* to me earlier and my only part in this was encouraging him to find out what was going on. That's all I know." Her eyes narrowed, firm. She was serious and seemed offended Tiel would hint as to their working both sides.

"I want to find out where this particle accelerator has gone," Riley said to Tiel. "It seems the damage done to the lower levels of Stake 47 isn't as bad as I thought given you were able to take inventory and find out if anything was missing."

"Some of the crates were fire and shock-proof. They have their advantage," Tiel said.

"Was anything else stolen?"

"No. This was obviously deliberate."

"Send Sophie and I back to the scene. Perhaps we could investigate."

"We already had a higher-level team comb through there."

"But what were they looking for?"

"They didn't find out who did it."

"But we know that they were using the Exo-gauntlets. Those were our suits. Stolen, but ours. Have you tried the trackers?"

"What do you think? Besides, I told you earlier they were disabled."

"Just asking." He put his hands on his hips. "Let Sophie and I go in and look around, see what might turn up. If we find something, it'll be the break we need. If not, then at least we left no stone unturned. Please?"

Sophie looked at Tiel, hopeful.

Tiel grimaced and took a long puff off his cigar. He exhaled the smoke and when it looked like he was going to speak, he took another puff. He turned his back to them and exhaled the plume of smoke. It rose around his head. He turned back around, his face peering through it. "You're going to need a team."

◆ ◆ ◆

EN ROUTE TO STAKE 47

Tiel's idea of a team made Riley wonder if the man took this operation seriously at all. It was dawn and there were four of them: himself, Sophie Jones, Grayson Wilder, and Nick Fox.

Great, he thought, *two hens amongst the roosters.* It had to be done, according to Tiel. Him and Sophie couldn't be trusted, not after what they pulled the other night.

The four were outfitted with Renosis-4 exo-skeletons. He knew he was adept at using them; so was Nick, who was in his early sixties. The man had seen more action than anyone between World War III *and* the Mech War. He also heard Nick did some touring elsewhere prior to WWIII, but wasn't sure where.

All four exos were in flight, heading toward Stake 47.

Sophie came on Riley's comm. "Feel like I'm being babysat."

"Yeah, well, we are," he said.

"Tiel can be merciless sometimes."

"Be thankful that this is all we're getting after breaking into his office last night. Obviously he cares about the particle accelerator and its recovery otherwise he never would've agreed to this or had been so revealing about it."

"Do the other two know what we're after?"

"Don't you remember the briefing?"

"I started to doze off, late night and all."

"They were advised of property having been stolen, but it's label was Crate 82A. They don't know of the contents, unless they were pulled aside when I wasn't there."

"Well, the crate isn't there anyway."

"You were awake for that part?"

"When Tiel said a recovery team was sent in and removed the items that were there and brought them back to 48 for safekeeping? Yeah."

"Going to need you on the ball." He checked his readouts. Stake 47 should be coming up under them in two minutes.

"Sorry for being human."

"You're an officer at Stake 48. You're not supposed to be human."

"Har har."

He smiled and adjusted the temperature controls inside the suit. He didn't remember setting the heat so high the last time he used it.

The four flew on in silence.

Nick came on the group comm. channel. "Stake 47 below us. Beginning descent."

Riley tilted the boosters and began angling downward. They broke through the clouds and Stake 47 came into view. As much he enjoyed the view from up here, he braced himself for what he might find at ground level.

There was work to do.

6

RETURNING HERE AFTER the operation went bust made Riley uncomfortable. Four innocent men had died down here, their bodies incinerated in the fire. At least whatever might have been left of them would've been carted off when the recovery team had swept through here.

It had been his fault.

The room was barren save for the light coming in through the hole in the roof, having been put there two days before when those Exo-gauntlets had busted through.

The four went to work, scanners on, lights shining from the arm units, bringing light blue glows of illumination to various parts of the room.

Sophie was off in a corner, scanning the walls. Nick was by the elevator shaft, checking things out there. Grayson was up by the rafters, carefully walking them and shining her light upon them.

In the middle of the room, Riley went over to where he remembered the men kneeling in front of the Exo-gauntlet. There was no sign of any remains. He set his scanners to detect any lingering heat trails. Since the scene was two days old, any heat signature left by the Exo-gauntlet's boosters would've dissipated by now. The flame from the fire would've only mildly distorted it as the boosters ran on a different heat spectrum. It was worth a look, anyway, but he turned up nothing. Next he pulled up the Exo-gauntlet's specs and got a readout of the different metals used in its construction. He had hoped that—as strong as the Exo-gauntlet's armor was—some microscopic particles might've flaked off and left a trail as the unit had traversed the room.

Nothing.

He walked the floor, running his scans throughout the main body of the room.

Grayson came on the comm., humming the tune to "Blue Suede Shoes." Then she said, "Sorry," and cut out.

Must've activated the channel by accident, Riley thought. Now the song was in his head.

He checked around some of the fallen rafters, hoping to find anything the pilots of the Exo-gauntlets might've left behind. Nothing but debris.

He went on the comm. "Whoever did this did a good job of covering their tracks."

"Not completely," Nick said.

Riley went over to him. Nick was shining a light on the floor. The cement was broken in the shape similar to the foot of an Exo-gauntlet.

"Yeah, so?" Riley said. The other two joined them.

"This is from impact," Nick said.

"You do know these things weigh a ton, right? Any landing from a high surface and, well, the ground's not going to hold up too well."

"Two things: one, these things have shock absorbers so while they're not as quiet as a mouse, they land with minimal damage. Two: look at the outline. That's an Exo-gauntlet all right, but along the outer arch is a rectangular shape. A modification had been made to it, distorting its imprint."

"A footprint," Grayson breathed.

"At least we have a way of identifying the unit," Sophie said.

Riley took a snapshot of the imprint. He knew the others would do the same so he cleared some room.

Orange flickering light lit up the room and he heard the soft whirring of rocket boosters getting closer behind them.

They weren't alone.

"We got company!" he shouted.

The four immediately got into evasive positioning and split off, taking cover where they could. Riley went for the fallen rafters, crouching in behind them and activated Visor-7. Several loud metallic thunks sounded, indicating whoever had just joined them had landed.

He scanned the room, turning on the night vision. Low thumps echoed as heavy exo-suit feet walked along the floor.

He got on the comm. "We need to do a headcount."

Grayson came on. "Taking a look. Nick, you see anything?"

"Not yet. I'm checking."

Sophie added, "I got two in the southeast corner. Exo-gauntlets."

Riley angled himself so his cannon was ready for anything that might appear from the shadows in front. He peered over the rafters. "I see two as well. Both Exo-gauntlets."

"That makes four," Grayson said.

"You can count," Nick said. "I spot three near the north side."

"I see one," Grayson said.

Riley searched for any more. "I got nothing aside from the two here."

"Same," Sophie said.

"Looks like we got eight," Nick said.

"You can count," Grayson said.

"Ha ha."

"Can the chatter, guys. We need to focus," Riley said.

He eyed the two Exo-gauntlets carefully. They were both on the prowl, moving about then stopping to look things over.

Looking for *them.*

"Should we hightail it out of here?" Grayson asked.

"Whoever these guys are," Nick said, "they're most likely those responsible. Commander Tiel would've informed us if he was sending others in with us. These guys also would've come on the comm. if they were friendlies. If we don't take them down, we might not ever get the information we need."

"Good call," Riley said. "Take it slow, gang. We're in an enclosed space, not the ideal place for a firefight. At least, nothing monumental. Try to keep it contained. If things escalate, take it outside."

"Roger," Grayson said.

"Got it," Sophie added.

Riley armed his cannon with a low-level plasma burst. It would be enough to knock the exos off their feet. Hopefully whoever was piloting them would panic, make a mistake. He took aim and sent off a blast to the one nearest him. The plasma burst hit it square in the chest and sent it flying back ten feet. It landed upright but teetered. Its partner immediately aimed its own cannon in his direction. He ducked back down behind the rafters.

The sound of gunfire burst on the air as his comrades started up with the others in the room.

Riley peered over the rafters again and sent another burst at the other exo. It seemed ready and formed its arms in front of it like an X and absorbed the blow, only skidding back a few feet. Using its raised arms like a self-imposed blind spot, Riley turned on the thrusters and shot up over the rafters, rose into the air in a sharp arc, then came down in front it. He used his own exo's arms like a sword and brought them down on the other exo's, knocking down its guard. He delivered a swift blow to the exo's head, staggering it. He spun around behind it and sent off another plasma burst, this one into the back of the exo's head. The suit went sprawling onto the floor. The other one was on its feet and barreling toward him. It slammed into him like a bull and sent him flying back. Just as he was getting back onto his feet, recovering, the other exo charged into him again and tumbled on top of him. Cannon aimed, it sent forth a barrage of bullets into Riley's armor.

Grunting, Riley brought his cannon arm in from the side and used it like a baseball bat, knocking the other's weapon away. He fired plasma bursts in quick succession, sending it off him.

Things were moving too quickly and to get a clear shot at the kill switch in the back of the head unit, like the mechs, would be near impossible. Riley was a good shot, but not *that* good.

Both of the enemy exos streamed in from the side, crashing into him and locking him in a dual bear hug. Activating his thrusters, Riley took them both into the air toward the bunker's roof. Up here, he caught a quick glimpse of the battle below.

Nick was in the corner, firing clean bursts of plasma energy as well, knocking back the attacking exo. One of the gauntlets was already down, just lying on the floor. He didn't notice if the pilot escaped or not. Perhaps he or she was dead.

Grayson had her hands full wrestling with another enemy exo while yet another closed in.

He searched for Sophie but didn't see her.

Inside the suit, a couple of sparks flew, indicating pressure from the outside as if the two exos clamping onto him were trying to squeeze him out like toothpaste from a tube.

He flew to the side of the building full tilt, slamming one of the exos against the wall. Hopefully the impact had been enough to scramble it. When it didn't let go, he did it again. Then a third time. Finally it released its grip and fell to the ground in a loud crash. He brought his cannon around against the other one and fired four plasma bursts, sending it off him.

The exo that fell didn't move on the ground.

Two down so far, it seemed.

Six left.

Riley arced the suit and flew toward the one he just shot off, which hovered in the air. It brought both hands around and slammed them into him. He tumbled backward through the air, the suit spinning. He activated his stabilizers, righted himself, then flew low then high, coming up underneath it. He slammed into it and crashed with it through the rafters and plowed it into the roof. Sparks flew again inside his suit and he hoped the damage wasn't too severe.

"Come on, guys, talk to me," he said as he let the enemy exo fall to the floor.

Three down.

"Took two out," Grayson said.

"Got one," Nick said.

That made six.

"In pursuit of one heading out the opening in the ceiling," Sophie said.

"Stay on it," Riley said. He scanned below and saw Grayson and Nick cornering the enemy exo. Both had their cannons raised at it. "Drop him."

Grayson fired. So did Nick. The plasma bursts sent the exo flying backward.

"I need you two to stay here," Riley said. "Radio Tiel. Update him. He's going to have to let more people in on this. A cleanup crew, even. Make sure the downed Exo-gauntlets stay down. If anyone tries to make a break for it, contain them. If they resist, handle as necessary."

"Copy," Nick said.

Riley flew off out the opening and got a lock on Sophie's tracker. She wasn't too far ahead, only a few kilometers.

"Sophie, do you read?" he asked.

"Roger. Still tailing him, going as fast as I can. He's got good maneuverability."

"Stay on him. I'm right behind you."

"The others?"

"Nick and Grayson are back at 47, minding the others. They'll get on the horn with Tiel and await orders."

"Good to know and—" She didn't finish.

"Sophie?"

Nothing.

7

THE MISSILE WAS headed straight for her.

Are you serious? Sophie thought.

She banked sharply to the left. The missile sped past. Relief washed over her. Suddenly, her sensors came alive and a monotone beeping let her know she wasn't out of the woods yet.

The missile had adjusted course and was back on her.

"Sophie!" It was Riley.

"Sorry, got sidetracked. He launched a target-seeking missile at me."

"Try to shake it."

"There's a reason they call it 'target-seeking,'" she said.

"This isn't the time for jokes. Try and lose it. I'll get there as soon as I can."

"Copy."

She went into evasive maneuver mode. At ten thousand feet, she had plenty of space to move around.

The missile seemed to be gaining speed. It was no doubt an upgrade to the enemy Exo-gauntlet because all the reading she had done on the suits never mentioned it had targeting ability. She banked right just as the missile was hot on her heels.

"Come on, not today. Can't die today," she said.

The missile sped past and went way ahead of her.

It wasn't enough. It adjusted course and was back on her. She arced upward, downward, left, right—the thing kept trailing her.

"I'm closing in," Riley said.

"That's nice. Have any ideas?"

"Aside from leading it down to a target below—which isn't an option—just one. Here's what we're going to do." He laid out the plan.

"Roger."

She angled upward, heading high into the sky. She tried to keep an eye on the escaping exo, but lost sight of it the higher she ascended. *Great. Lost him!*

The missile followed her a couple hundred feet behind.

"Let me know when to stop," Sophie said. She gave the thrusters everything her suit had and went higher.

"A little more," Riley said.

She kept going up.

"Now!" he shouted.

She lurched forward then dove downward in a sharp arc. The missile sped past. As she flew downward, Riley flew past her in his suit. From her interior sensors, she saw him launch a heat seeker from his suit. A few seconds later, the heat seeker connected with the missile and a loud explosion rocked the air as the thing went off.

"Riley!" she shouted. No reply. "Riley!"

"Tumbling. Can't. Talk."

She turned her suit around and watched as Riley fell from the sky, orange flame and black smoke from the exploded missile above him.

"Hit your stabilizers," she said.

"Trying. Getting jostled in here."

"Try harder!"

He spiraled to the earth below.

As she watched him fall, she saw a yellow spark in the distance: the thrusters from the escaping Exo-gauntlet.

After hesitating a moment, she flew after it.

Riley was on his own.

♦ ♦ ♦

Riley's exo-suit spun out of control as he tumbled through the air. He pulled his hands up through the arm cavities and brought them into the torso of the suit and pulled down on the cover to the manual control panel. The stabilizers weren't responding and while they could be controlled through the arm sockets, he only had one choice at the moment. He reached for the manual power control and activated the lever. Auto-functions were now off-line and it was up to him to pilot the suit manually. He shut the suit down and all the power went off, including visualization to the outside.

He was falling blind.

He counted a quick ten seconds then pulled on the lever. A moment later, the interior of the suit lit up and began running its reboot program.

"Come on, hurry!" he shouted.

It'd be a few seconds before things were on-line again and he hoped by rebooting the system the stabilizers would reactivate.

He slid his hands back into the arm sockets and felt around for the controls. Once locating them, he struck the appropriate button and the thrusters ignited. He immediately righted, fell for another second, then with a violent jolt shot upward.

Riley looked to the ground below then checked the altimeter readout on his screen. He'd been at just nine hundred feet. A few seconds more and he wouldn't have recovered.

Sweating, catching his breath, he locked onto Sophie's tracker and sped toward her.

♦ ♦ ♦

Sophie kept her distance from the escaping exo, hoping she was far enough behind she'd be out of its immediate line of sight.

Where was he going?

"Riley, do you copy?" she asked.

It took a second, but he responded. "I'm here. Barely."

"You okay?"

"I'll live." Then, "What do you see?"

"He's flying steady. I'm assuming he's heading back to his nest."

"Any indication as to where?"

"Outskirts of the city. He's flying north, straight toward the Old Zone."

"What if he's going past it?"

"There's nothing past it. At least, nothing that I know of."

"Stay on him. I'll try and catch up as soon as possible."

"Roger."

She kept flying after the Exo-gauntlet, hoping that it'd lead her right to whoever stole the particle accelerator. She just hoped she wouldn't have to face them alone. She radioed Tiel.

"Jones?" Tiel said.

"It's me. Listen, I got a guy heading north toward the Old Zone. Riley got delayed but is coming to meet me."

"I spoke to the others and I'm sending a crew in to detain those still alive."

"How many causalities?"

"Unconfirmed."

"Wouldn't bringing others in blow the whole thing about you-know-what wide open?"

"It'll be on a need-to-know basis. I'm logging into your visor's feed now so I'll be seeing what you see."

"Copy."

Riley came on. "I'm right behind you. Slow up a little, if you can."

"Only a little," she said, and made the adjustment.

Far ahead, the escaping exo was a tiny black dot on the horizon. It finally looked like it was beginning to dip down toward a range of hills.

She never took her eyes off it, even when Riley caught up beside her a couple of minutes later.

"See it?" she asked.

"Looking." A few seconds later, "Got him."

The two flew on. The black dot grew larger so they altered their course slightly and flew higher, hoping that any scanners down below were only tracking things near ground level instead of in the sky.

The black dot stopped and, a couple minutes more, grew large enough for Sophie's visual sensors to get a lock on it. Now she could maintain her distance and simply magnify what her visor was picking up. Looking on the visor screen, she saw the Exo-gauntlet land at the base of a large hill near a smattering of large rocks. It stopped, waited a moment, then disappeared between two of the boulders.

"Wait, where'd he go?" Sophie asked.

"Inside," Riley said.

Hovering high above the hill, they reported what they saw to Tiel in case he wasn't minding the feed.

"Yeah, I know. I'm monitoring from here. That area is supposed to be a dead zone, leftover from the war,"

Commander Tiel said. "It's off-limits to civilians and even our personnel rarely go over there."

"What's there?" Riley asked.

"Nothing. Supposed to be, anyway. Now it seems like you two found something."

"What should we do?"

"Can you get a closer look?"

"I'm sure we could," Sophie said. "But you do realize we're probably floating above enemy territory here and could even be walking into a trap."

"Could be. I also don't want to send in an entire fleet of exos and let them know we know where they are. 'They' could be anybody and in any number. Try and get a closer look and report back to me. I need to monitor the cleanup and see how Wilder and Fox are doing."

"Understood," Sophie said. To Riley, "You got my back?"

"Always."

8

THE FOREST

THEY SCANNED THE area below: hills and rocks. Most of the foliage was a trampled mess, the area having not fully recovered since the war. Mech-bots had trampled the whole area during the various battles. Any wildlife—Riley doubted there'd be any and if there was, it'd be animals that could survive amongst fallen trees.

No readings came off the hills. If there was a base inside, it was well-concealed.

"We should go lower, but do it further out," he said.

"All right," Sophie said.

They flew a kilometer out from the hill then slowly descended into the forest of fallen trees and trampled bushes, cannons at the ready.

"We're too close," Sophie said.

"Keep your sensors on high alert. Perhaps they'll pick up if we're being tracked."

"That's assuming whomever we're dealing with has that kind of tech."

"We don't know what we're dealing with or how advanced their network is."

The two moved through the woods, stepping over fallen trees, scanning the area, cannons always ready to fire at a moment's notice.

"And when we get there?" Sophie asked.

"I suppose we can just knock," Riley said.

"Not funny. Not now."

"Sorry." He had to mind the playful banter. They were still on a mission, after all.

He hoped that while they traversed the woods, he could make up for lost time with Sophie. Ever since graduating from the academy, they had spent less and less time together. For a time, they were in separate divisions and on opposite shifts. Aside from the occasional pass by each other in the corridors of Stake 47 back when it was active, they rarely saw each other. There was one mission during the war they had in common, however: a recovery mission for a downed mech-bot in the heart of downtown. Two teams went in to pull out a pilot and his two co-pilots. They had got there too late and while the mech-bot was fallen over, the pilots trapped, one of the enemy mechs had come in and blown the thing wide open. Only one of the co-pilots survived. Half of him, actually, and he was forever confined to a wheelchair after that. Riley had been team leader, with Sophie and Greg second in command. While the mission had been all business, it was good to see her again and they were able to get a few words in that were non-work-related before rushing to the co-pilot's aid.

Later, Sophie had been reassigned though the two were in the same division. While they didn't run missions together, he got to see her at briefings and in the mess hall.

As they walked through the forest, Riley wondered if Sophie ever thought of him or missed their time together at the academy. There was no real way to ask her so all he could do was simply be her friend in the here and now and hope the bond they shared still ran strong despite years of limited time together.

They came to a series of enormous fallen trees, their branches and limbs tangled together like a wooden spider web.

"We'll have to go around," he said.

"Or we could just fly over," she replied. She activated her thrusters and started her ascent.

"Sophie, don't!" Plasma rays came in streaking from the side hot and fast. "You'll call attention to yourself," he finished. *Great.*

All but one missed her and she was knocked from her flight and fell on the other side. Riley took his suit along the gigantic trunk of a tree then stopped before rounding its rear. He set his scanners on full alert and surveyed the forest.

Nothing came up. Whoever was out there was good at hiding, using the mess of the enormous fallen trees to distort any signals they gave off.

Cannon raised, Riley slowly rounded the base of the tree then headed back along it toward where he thought Sophie had fallen.

"You okay?" he asked into the comm.

He heard the whirring of her suit as it was most likely righting itself and standing up. "Roger. Just didn't see that coming."

"You have to be more careful. Keep your eyes peeled."

"Copy that. Lesson learned."

He met up with her and they stood back-to-back, weapons at the ready.

"Whoever's out here doesn't want us here," he said.

"No kidding. Was it another exo?"

"No idea. The shot came out of the woods. Scanners didn't pick up anything."

A few moments later, she said, "I can't detect anything either. Retreat?"

"No. We keep moving. If things get too hot, we go straight up and out."

"Okay."

They started again in the direction of the hills. Clearly they were onto something. Less than a minute later, another plasma ray came streaking in from the side. It struck Riley on the right, knocking his suit into Sophie's, sending them both tumbling to the left.

From overhead, more rays shot in, coming down like plasma rain.

"Run!" Riley said and the two thundered further into the woods. The rays deluged down behind them, their exos barely keeping one step ahead.

"Take off?" Sophie asked.

A shadow streaked by some twenty-five feet to the right. "I see 'im. One of them, anyway. I'm going after him. Keep heading forward."

"Copy."

Riley veered off to the right. His scanner picked up what appeared to be another exo darting up northeast ahead of him. Cannon out, he fired into the woods. Plasma rays fired back. Riley sent off another burst in the direction they came from then adjusted his own cannon to send off the same kind of rays.

"Want a firefight?" he said. "You got it."

The exo-suits were heavily armored. Plasma bursts were meant to disrupt, not kill. Only if fired in rapid succession in the same spot would they breach the armor and make their way in. Whoever was firing at him, at least at the moment, might be interested in taking him alive.

He caught sight of a black exo running in the woods ahead of him, stopping to turn and fire, then keeping on.

His focus on the one ahead of him, he didn't see the one coming in from the side until it was too late.

◆ ◆ ◆

Sophie discharged several plasma bursts toward the black exo that dropped down in front of her from a series of criss-crossing fallen trees. She connected dead on and sent the other suit reeling back. She took a quick moment and tried to identify the model, but the black finish on it only added to the shadows between the metallic crevasses, making the features hard to determine.

The enemy exo raised both arms and gauntlet barrels rolled out the side of its forearms. A barrage of bullets blasted at her, their rapid impact making her shake inside the suit.

She quickly armed her micro rockets. From her shoulders, a small compartment opened up on each of them and she let the exo have one from each side. They shot off and connected, hitting the enemy exo square in the chest and exploded on impact. The enemy suit went flying back, still firing its weapon as it landed backwards on the ground. Sparks flew, the weapon stopped, and the exo lay still.

Sophie came over to it, her cannon drawn, and took a closer look. The front shell of the enemy's exo-suit was blown open, part of the metal twisted, its corner lodged deep into the pilot's chest.

Dead.

She sighed, hating the idea of taking a life. She continued on through the forest.

♦ ♦ ♦

Riley had been taken to the ground as the enemy exo crashed onto him. It rained down its armored forearms, smashing into Riley's hull. The loud, low drumming of metal on metal exploded in Riley's ears.

"Get. Off!" he shouted and shoved his cannon right into the exo's head. He sent off three plasma bursts in quick succession and sent the thing off him. He quickly got to his feet and sent four more into the thing's head, blowing it off. If the enemy's suit was anything like his own, the pilot's head would've been partly behind the exo's and, well, there was no coming back from what he just did to it.

He scanned the forest for the exo he was just tailing.

He lost it.

Another barrage of fire came from behind the fallen trees.

Riley took off into the forest.

This little battle seemed far from over.

9

SOPHIE WAS UNDER heavy fire. The plasma rays streaked in from all directions and it took all she had to maneuver her exo-suit side-to-side, stop, jump forward, even roll it a few times behind the cover of fallen trees.

She came up to another spider web of tangled branches, these ones all clumped together like a giant, haphazard beaver dam. She got on the other side of it and took cover.

Can't stay here too long. I'm a sitting duck! she thought. "Riley, do you copy?"

"Kind of busy here. Where are you?"

"Aren't you tracking? I see you're east of me."

"Sorry. Occupied." She could hear plasma fire coming through on his comm. "I got you. Can you—" More fire.

"Riley!"

He didn't come back on. He was like that: sometimes too focused on the task at hand to be mindful of anything else. It was what made him a good leader and a good soldier. It was a trait he possessed that she admired. Sometimes, she knew, she took things too lightly, even when it was time to put on a straight face and get down to business. Maybe one day she'd grow up.

Could be today.

The branches above her blasted apart, raining down woodchips and bark. She got moving and headed deeper into the woods. Had the mech-bots that had trampled through here during the war flattened everything completely, it would be much simpler to see where the enemy exos were hiding, but with the trees fallen over cracked at the trunks at different angles and at different heights, she might as well be in a fully matured forest.

A streak of black on her left caught her attention. She got low and fired her cannon. The blast sent a log up in chips.

"Come on, where are you?" she said. "Riley?" Still nothing. "You know, you should answer when people are talking to you." What was with that guy?

Just chill out, stay calm. Keep your head on. No sense getting up in arms over— Plasma rays came in from the front, taking her exo's legs out from under her. She planted face first, the view in her visor suddenly shifting from fallen trees to grass and dirt.

She got up and immediately returned fire . . . and hit nothing.

Sudden impact from behind sent her bolting forward inside her suit, slamming her back to the ground. Blows rained down on her from behind, throwing her off her game. She had to remember her training, especially the one exercise where cadets were told to stay still and relax their bodies inside the suit while the training suit had been hoisted up on a set of cables and sent spinning, was tugged back and forth, side-to-side, up-and-down, the goal to still stay focused enough to shoot at holographic targets revolving around them.

The key was to not pay any mind to the impacts, but to concentrate on the task at hand: in this case, getting her exo to safety.

She shoved her suit's metal hands into the dirt, worked the controls so they dug deep, the pulled back on the arms so she could abruptly scoot herself forward along the dirt. It worked, and what was no doubt an exo on her back slid onto her legs. She threw on her thrusters, sending a blast of flame and heat at the exo, knocking it off while she shot forward along the ground. She managed to veer around a couple fallen trees before plowing headlong into the fat tree trunk of another. It stopped her like a brick wall and sparks flew inside her suit. She hit her head, bashed her face; buzzing filled her ears.

Come on, not now. You can't pass out. Her head throbbed and she could still hear the echo of the low drone of impact in her skull.

"Get. Up." She got herself upright. Her visor was cracked and the readouts skipped on and off in flashes of static.

She turned the suit around and two quick successive plasma blasts sent her back against the tree trunk.

Three black exos flashed in and out of view in her visor. One came forward and struck her with its metal fist.

◆ ◆ ◆

Riley ran between the bullets firing at him. He felt bad for not getting back to Sophie, but he needed his concentration on the here and now. It was either that, or risk distraction that could lead to death.

He saw a black exo bounding in from the right. He fired at it and knocked it down. Another came in from the left. He shot this one down as well. The bursts would be enough to slow them, but not enough to incapacitate them.

Quickly, he locked onto Sophie's tracker and started heading in her direction.

"Sophie, do you copy?" He fired at the exo chasing him from behind. The plasma burst sent it staggering. He shot again, sending it back down when it tried to get up.

Activating the micro rockets on his shoulders, he stopped and pivoted the suit's torso in its direction and sent off a half dozen of them to the exo over there. Tree trunks and branches blew up and he was pretty sure he heard the rocket strike metal before exploding.

The one on the left came in hard and fast, sending bullets his way. He faced it and unloaded the rest of the micro rockets. Explosions rang out as they hit paydirt and the black exo was blown away.

Rapid, heavy footfalls sounded behind him. He threw on the thrusters and shot straight up while the black exo raced past him below. He shot plasma rays at it from behind, one after the other, cutting into it. The exo went down. Riley hovered above it then cut off the thrusters and dropped straight down, the heavy steel feet of his suit slamming into the exo's back, crushing whoever was within.

"Sophie," he said, and started after her.

Thank goodness for a moment's reprieve, he thought as he made his way through the woods in her direction.

"Sophie?" he said into his comm. Still nothing. "Come on, answer me!"

She didn't.

He stopped short when the tracker said he should be almost upon her, then he saw Sophie outside her suit, walking with her hands on her head in front of three black exos. Her exo-suit was tethered to the back of one of them.

"Not again," he said, thinking back to Stake 47 and the hostages. "Okay. Stay calm. Let's think. Three of them. One of you." The enemy exos were situated as such that one was directly behind her, cannon aimed at her back, the two others behind it in a triangle formation. "They're no doubt in communication with each other, which means they're probably aware their comrades have fallen." *Are there any more?* The woods seemed quiet. For now, anyway.

The key here would be to get in between Sophie and the hostile exos. Were they aware he was watching them? Were they counting on him to come rushing in and rescuing her? Regardless, he couldn't leave her.

If he tried to take all three on at once, there was a good chance Sophie would get caught in the crossfire and without the armor of her exo-suit, she'd be as good as dead.

"What to do, what to do . . ." he breathed.

Then it hit him. It was the only option.

Riley stayed put and let Sophie and the exos move past him until he was able to get himself in behind them.

Slowly, he started moving forward, cannon ready for any who might be watching him from afar. He once again checked his scanner for hostiles and came up empty.

Fortunately, because Sophie was on foot, she moved slower than she would've in the suit and had to take her time navigating all the fallen trees. It enabled Riley to gain ground relatively quickly. He did his best to be quiet and watch where he stepped. When he was about twenty-five feet behind them, he took a deep breath, then activated his thrusters and took off into the air, heading toward them, only flying high enough that he would just clear the exos' heads.

He was upon them in no time and in an instant he came down between Sophie and the exo behind her, blasted the exo, then took Sophie in his arms and headed straight up. In a couple of seconds they'd be in the clear. In a couple of seconds—

Plasma rays shot him from behind and sent him lurching forward. Sophie screamed. They were only some fifteen feet from the ground, ten from the tops of the fallen tree trunks. Another blast sent him spinning with her in his arms and he lost control. The two hit the ground. He was careful to at least land on his back with Sophie above him so he wouldn't crush her.

He skidded to a halt and turned the thrusters off.

The three exos hurried over to him, weapons aimed. Two more came in from the sides.

So much for his daring rescue.

10

NICK SIGHED. HE and Grayson had monitored the fallen enemy exos until the cleanup crew arrived. Now, the place filled with a dozen men, he hoped they could finally get some answers.

Out of all the attackers, two had survived, the men pulled from their exos, and taken into custody.

Cuffed, they were led over to the side while a few of the crew examined the enemy exo-suits. Nick and Grayson were put on watch detail, making sure the men didn't try anything funny while they waited for transport.

Grayson was still in her suit. Nick was out of his, a Colt .45 aimed at the two men. It was an old weapon—an antique—but one he still favored. Some made fun of him for still using it, but his motto was if it ain't broke, don't try to fix it.

The two men stood there, cuffed hands in front of them. One looked Latino, the other black. Judging by their clothes—simple gray sweaters and matching cargo pants—they appeared to be part of some rag tag unit instead of a formal brigade. Then again, looks could be deceiving.

The black fellow was clearly unhappy and wore his frown with seeming pride. The Latino man kept his eyes to the floor.

"You guys want to start talking now about what you were doing here," Nick asked, "or would you rather wait until you're all warm and cozy in a cement cell?"

They didn't reply.

I hate this, the waiting game, he thought. In the old days, they got things done. Captured an enemy soldier? You broke him down on the spot, got what you needed, then dealt with him accordingly.

Grayson seemed new at this. She simply stood there, quiet. Why Commander Tiel had put a rookie like her on their team, he didn't know. There had to be a reason. Tiel was usually very deliberate in his decisions.

The Latino shifted on his feet, moving his lips out then in, out then in.

What was he chewing on? Gum?

"Spit it out," Nick said.

The guy kept moving his lips.

"I said, spit it out!" He aimed the weapon at the man's head.

The Latino took a step back, straightened his head, then parted his lips. In between his teeth was a metal cylinder.

It was flashing red.

"Look out!" Nick shouted and grabbed the black guy, pulling him away. "Grayson!"

He dragged the enemy soldier away as the flashing cylinder let off a rapid tone.

The explosion sent a fireball outward. Nick took the black guy to the floor and laid on top of him. He glanced over his shoulder. Grayson had taken her exo to safety. The Latino had been blown to smithereens. Other members of the crew rushed over. One uniformed officer helped Nick and the captured soldier to their feet.

"No, stay back!" Nick said, arm outstretched. He put the barrel of his weapon against the man's temple. "You got one, too?" He pressed the barrel against his skin harder. "Huh?"

The man was silent.

"If you're ready to die, just let me know. All I need to do is squeeze."

Was that fear in the man's eyes? Maybe he didn't carry the same resolve as his comrade.

The man worked his lips. Nick kept his arm out, keeping his fellow soldiers at bay. "Spit. It. Out. I'm warning you."

The man pushed his lips in and out like his friend had. Slowly, he brought his hands up to his mouth.

"No fast moves," Nick said.

Putting his palms to his lips, the man puffed his cheeks then sucked them in. A metal cylinder came out and landed in his hands. Nick grabbed it, looked it over. It wasn't flashing.

To the man, he said, "You just saved your life."

◆ ◆ ◆

INSIDE THE HILL

Riley and Sophie had been blindfolded once they arrived at the base of the hills. Now, outside his suit and walking inside what felt like a stone corridor, Riley'd never know how they got inside. He heard Sophie breathing beside him as they were shoved forward. He hoped she'd stay calm. He needed to get access to his exo-suit so he could call into base and let them know where they were. Most likely it was tethered to the back of one of the enemy exo's like Sophie's had been.

The cold steel of an exo forearm pushed against his left shoulder, steering him to the right. He had tried to keep a mental log of the turns they took so far, but started getting mixed up some nine turns in.

All he could do was be patient as they led him ever deeper into the heart of the hill.

◆ ◆ ◆

STAKE 48

Commander Tiel came into the room, cigar between his teeth. Nick didn't mind the smell, but Grayson made a face. The three of them were on one side of a two-way mirror, the black man who manned the enemy exo sitting in a chair behind a small table on the other side.

Tiel had a data pad in his hand, scrolling through its screens with his thumb. "This the only guy, huh?"

"Yes, sir," Nick said. "The other one blew himself up."

Tiel simply raised his eyebrows up and down: uh-huh.

Grayson, arms crossed, inched over behind Tiel and snuck a peek at the data pad from over his shoulder.

"Do you mind?" Tiel said.

"Sorry. Any idea who he is?" she asked. She curled a lock of her chin-length black hair behind her ear.

"That's what we're about to find out. You two stay here. I'll talk to him. Mind his vitals and let me know via earpiece if something jumps."

"Yes, sir," Grayson said.

Tiel stubbed out his cigar in an ashtray on a small round table then went to the door beside the mirror. He entered the room with the man and closed the door behind him.

Both Nick and Grayson went up to the mirror for a front row seat.

"Think he'll break him?" Grayson asked.

"He's got to," Nick said. "We need to know who we're dealing with."

♦ ♦ ♦

Tiel sat down across from the man. "Can I get you anything? Water? Coffee? Suicide cylinder?"

The man simply sat there, a grimace on his face.

"I see," Tiel said and scanned the data pad. "Says here you and seven others attacked my men."

"We were defending ourselves," the man said, his voice gruff.

"That's not what I heard. You guys came in and let them have it."

"That's your side of the story."

"I tend to trust my people."

"Maybe that's your mistake."

Well, at least he's talkative, Tiel thought. *Nick said this guy didn't look like he was willing to go through with blowing himself up like his friend was. Perhaps he'll blow the whistle on who he's working for?* "How about I get you that coffee?"

The man straightened in his chair.

"Tea?" Tiel said.

He shook his head.

"You seem a young fellow," Tiel said. "I got you pegged at twenty-two, twenty-three." The man appeared no more than twenty-five. "Want to tell me why you guys were at one of our facilities? You realize that's trespassing."

"Just doing my job."

"And who's your employer?"

"None of your concern."

He set the data pad down at the far corner of the table, out of eyeshot of the man. Tiel folded his hands and leaned forward in his seat. "It *is* my concern. You and the others were manning Exo-gauntlets. Do you know what those are? Yes, they do have a name."

"Those were our suits."

"So you were told. Did anyone, wherever you're from, show you where they got them? Did you guys build your own?"

He didn't reply.

Good. Now he's talking to me. Sometimes the non-replies were more telling than actual words. Clearly this guy—unless he was a good actor—was just hired help, somehow, some time ago roped in with the wrong people. Just do your job, don't ask any questions.

"As law enforcement, we have the right to hold you as long as we want," Tiel said. "If you cooperate, we can see about making your stay here shorter. If you don't, you're going to be here for a very long time."

"Makes no difference to me."

"See," Tiel said, "I think it does. You don't strike me as the kind of guy who really wants to be here. Sure, you might put on a show, a bit of bravado, try and make me think you're tough, but deep down I think you want to go back to your family."

"Don't have any family."

Nick's voice came in over Tiel's earpiece: "He's telling the truth, so far."

Tiel didn't give any sign he heard him. The scanner mounted in the top corner of the room monitored the prisoner's life signs, including heart rate. He was glad Nick was keeping an eye on it.

"Well," Tiel said, "maybe not family, but those you're close to back at your . . . base?"

He didn't say anything.

"I'm going to be straight with you," Tiel said. "I need to know who sent you in to ambush my men. You don't even need to tell me your name. But, see, we don't like it when things are stolen from us and those Exo-gauntlets didn't belong to you."

The man's eyes did a little dance. Was he getting scared?

"Or," Tiel said, "I can send you back, no harm, no foul." He paused. "Maybe a little harm. You see, when you came in here and they searched you, one of my people placed a micromb inside you. Do you know what a micromb is?"

Nick came on. "His heart rate jumped when you said that."

The man slightly shook his head.

"A micromb is a mini bomb, kind of like the one your friend used to kill himself, kind of like the one you spat out. You don't strike me as the kind of guy with a death wish. The beauty of a micromb is it's small, so small that you need a special scanner to even detect it, but, boy, do they pack a wallop. Ever see a grenade go off? Kind of like that, but more localized. We use them to plant explosives in hard-to-reach places. Keeps things undetected. They can be remote-detonated. There is one inside you now. You can't detect it, you can't pass it, you just have to live with it, knowing that at any moment we can use it."

Nick said, "His heart's beating quick."

"You lie," the man whispered.

"Would you like a demonstration?" Tiel asked. "I can show you."

The man sat perfectly still. He had him.

"Who are you working for?" Tiel said.

"They'll kill me, if I talk."

"That's if you go back to them, and that's if they know you talked."

"I won't say anything."

Nick said, "Press harder. His heart is moving at a good clip."

Tiel could see the sweat forming on the man's brow. He just needed to put him over the edge. "Come here." Tiel got up and grabbed the man by the arm. "I want to show you how this works."

The man resisted. Tiel tightened his grip, squeezing his fingers hard into the man's biceps. With a violent jerk, he tugged the man away from the table then kicked the table across the room where it crashed into the corner. He dragged the man back over to it and produced a small piece of metal the size of a watch battery and slapped it down on the table. With another forceful yank, he pulled the man over to the opposite side of the room. From his pocket, Tiel pulled out a flat, metal rectangle, keeping most of it concealed in his hand.

"Want to see? We need to stay over here because the blast will no doubt blow that table apart and send the debris flying. We might even get hit. I want to show you a demonstration on how the micromb works. Ready for some noise?"

"You wouldn't," the man said.

"This is my room. I'm the boss down here. I can do whatever I want."

"Please don't."

"No, really, you need to see this," Tiel said. He brought the metal rectangle near the man's ear. "Can you hear it ticking?"

The man shook his head.

"Maybe you aren't listening closely enough?" Tiel scooped his arm under the man's and bent him over in an arm bar. He put the metal rectangle near the man's ear again. "Hear it now?"

The man still shook his head. Tiel bent him forward further and pulled up on the arm. He didn't even bother putting the rectangle by the man's ear this time and only just pulled up on his arm, forcing the elbow joint to start bending the wrong way. "How about now?"

"No!" The man groaned.

"Fine. Then you'll just have to see this go off. I'm going to do that micromb over there then I'm going to do the one inside you. Ready?"

"Don't!"

"Set."

"Please don't!"

"Okay, here we go! Three, two—"

"Manta Six! Manta Six!"

Tiel torqued the man's arm a final time then threw him to the ground. "You better start talking."

WHEN TIEL CAME back into the room behind the mirror, he had a grave look on his face.

"You got him to spill everything," Nick said. "That micromb trick worked."

"It was a trick?" Grayson said.

Tiel flashed her the metal rectangle in his hand. It was his zippo.

"But the micromb?" Grayson said, pointing to the mirror.

"It was a broken snap from my uniform."

"Well played."

Nick rested his arm up on the heart rate monitor, the other hand on his hip. He replayed Tiel's conversation with Curt—the man's name, it turned out—over in his mind.

Tiel had shoved Curt onto the table, forcing him to sit on it with his back against the wall. He paced in front of him as he spoke.

"Start talking," Tiel had said.

Curt took a deep breath then let it out slowly. "There was supposed to be no evidence to link us to taking . . . they never told me what it was. What was it?"

"None of your concern."

"Well, there was supposed to be no evidence. That place was to be taken to the ground. I was part of a team to plant explosives, a simple get-in-get-out mission. We didn't count on running into your crew."

"I'm surprised at you. You really think we'd leave the place unattended or, at the very least, not check up on it?"

"It didn't occur to me but, probably, to those who sent me."

"You have still to tell me who they are. Where are you from? Who do you answer to?"

"I can't say."

"You can't say or you don't know?"

"I don't know."

"You're lying." Tiel pulled out the Colt .45 and aimed it at him. Nick had liked the man's style. "You have to give me more."

"In return?"

"I don't blow off your kneecaps."

Curt swallowed. "Manta Six."

Tiel's eyes went wide.

"I see you know them."

"I'm aware of who they are."

"They're still in play. *We're* still in play."

"Not for long."

"Don't be too sure. There's much more going on than you're aware. You think you guys have control of the city just because you patrol it in tidy little uniforms, have some exos and even walk the streets with mech-bots? Think again."

"Don't give me that guff," Tiel said. "You're a kid. Whatever they told you to say if you were captured, skip it. Talk to me straight or this gun here is going to start doing the talking for you."

Curt folded his hands and began slowly twiddling his thumbs. When he stopped, he said, "The war's not over. Never was. Was only put on hold."

"Manta Six isn't big enough to fight us."

"Manta Six is the leader. There are more. Way more."

"Have you seen them? Have you seen the troops?"

Curt didn't reply.

Tiel fired off a round, skimming Curt's foot, the bullet pinging the table leg. Curt jumped. "No, no! Haven't seen them! Heard rumors."

"Where?"

"The hills, north of the city. We're headquartered there."

"Why did you break into Stake 47?"

"I didn't. Another team did. I told you, I was part of bringing it to the ground. Nothing more." He took a breath. "What was taken?"

"None of your business."

"If you tell me, maybe I can help."

"I don't want your help other than to tell me anything else you know. Who's your commanding officer?"

Curt kept quiet. Why was he waffling between being helpful then acting as if he was trying to prove a point with his silence?

Tiel fired off another round, this one skimming the other foot. The table jerked beneath Curt from the bullet's impact.

"Davis. Captain Davis," Curt said.

Tiel grimaced. "Davis, huh? Does he have a first name?"

"Jarod."

"Who else do you answer to?"

When Tiel wrapped up and came back into the small room, Nick was glad it was over. His commander had scared the kid good and Curt had offered up a list of names.

"Do you know any of them?" Nick asked Commander Tiel.

"No, but we have the conversation recorded. We'll run the names across all known databases and see what turns up."

"This Manta Six," Grayson said, "what is it?"

"People you don't want to mess with," Tiel said. He went over to the comm. on the wall and radioed in a couple of officers to come and collect Curt. They'd be here in a moment.

"Curt said the war was never over," Nick said. "Wonder what he meant by that?"

"First impression is that it was a false surrender. The men we took were just patsies. The real players stayed back, bided their time. Now they're surfacing again. The assault and theft on Stake 47 was their first move."

"Any idea what their second might be?" Grayson asked.

The door to the interrogation room buzzed and two armed officers entered, grabbed Curt, and escorted him out. He'd be taken to the brig and left there until he answered for what he did. He'd also be available for any further questioning.

"Their next move could be anything, Wilder," Tiel said. He eyed Nick.

Nick knew full well Tiel knew he was aware of Manta Six. They had been an important faction during the war and acted as not only intelligence for the enemy side, but also bred a fleet of highly-skilled exo warriors. Their mech-bots were also nothing to shake a stick at. It seemed, given how the enemy exos had fallen and Curt's capture, that their current exo warriors weren't up to snuff. Or, it was also possible those sent in to destroy Stake 47 weren't as skilled as the warriors who might be back at base.

"Curt said they're located in the hills," Nick said. "That area's been a dead zone since the war ended . . . er . . . was put on hold."

"Hiding in plain sight, it seems," Tiel said. "Connor and Jones are there. Can't be good."

"What do we do?" Grayson asked.

Tiel pulled out a fresh cigar, lit it, and exhaled a thick plume of smoke. "We're going to have to let more people in on this. This is no longer a small operation. Manta Six is operative."

♦ ♦ ♦

Grayson and Nick had been assigned to check in with Riley and Sophie. Grayson didn't mind working with Nick. He was a seasoned vet, after all, and knew how to take charge.

They entered the Combat Monitoring Room and went to the appropriate screens on the monitors.

"Riley, come in. This is Stake 48. Do you copy?" Grayson said.

The line was dead.

"Try again," Nick said.

"Riley, this is Stake 48, come in, please," she said.

Nothing.

Grayson switched channels. "Sophie, this is Stake 48. Do you copy? Please respond."

Her line was dead as well.

Nick sat down at a monitoring station and began tapping the keypad in front of it. "Trackers are still active," he said. He hit a few more keys.

"Sophie, this is Grayson. Do you copy?" Still nothing. To Nick: "I can't raise them."

"They're in the hills," he said, "and I'm willing to bet they found themselves in a bunch of trouble."

12

One Week Later . . .

THE MILITANTS WERE playing the intimidation game. That was the only reason Riley and Sophie weren't dead. Each day that passed meant they were one day closer to finally being made an example of. They shared neighboring cells, each barred and separated by a thick wall of concrete. For the past week a pair of men would come into one of their cells and beat the tar out of them while the other one listened. Then they'd leave without a word. Riley had taken three beatings, so had Sophie.

Listening as they slapped her around and delivered blow after blow to her body twisted Riley's stomach every time. The last one, the way he heard her gasp for breath and throw up what had to be a couple cups of blood made him wish he could break the bars down and teach those guys a lesson. Instead, he could only sit on the bunk and mentally take each blow with her and, later, whisper her words of comfort.

Riley paced the tiny cell which ran only six by eight. It seemed to be modeled after the old jail cells from early in the century.

If the pattern of the past week had been any indicator, soon the two men would return, enter his cell, and make worse his already-broken nose and then some.

"I can hear you breathing," Sophie whispered from the next cell.

Riley went to the side of the bars closest to her. "I guess I'm not as tough as I thought I was."

"No one is."

"Just getting myself ready."

"What do they want?"

"We've already been over this. They're trying to scare us. The only reason we're still alive is they think we have something to offer them. They would've killed us in the forest had we been worthless."

Sophie groaned. "My ribs hurt."

"I know." He rubbed his leg. He had a welt there the size of a fist and even the material of his pants brushing against it made it sting.

"We have to get out of here," she said.

"I know. Got any ideas?"

"None."

"Come on, you're the sneaky one. Remember what we did to that guard back at the base?" He could imagine her smile.

"If only it were that simple."

Maybe it was because he was rattled, but he realized Sophie had a point. It *should* be that simple. They were trained soldiers. Trained not to roll over and give into an enemy, but also to outsmart them.

"Man, I'm hungry," Sophie said.

"My stomach stopped growling two days ago," he replied. They hadn't been given anything aside from water since they got here. Which reminded him— He went over to the cup by the foot of his bunk and took a sip. He was trying to ration it in case they decided to take that away from them, too.

He came back to the bars. "We need to hang in there, Sophie."

"I know. I'm surprised no one's come for us."

"Maybe they tried, but ran into trouble outside this place."

"Or maybe word was sent out we were dead and that's why nothing's happened."

"Then they'll be in for a big surprise when we return."

She sighed. "I don't think this place is heavily guarded."

"You told me."

"I know. Just saying it again. Makes me feel better. When they brought us here, I don't recall hearing a lot of doors or the beeping of swipe cards. Maybe two or three. Can't remember right now. Head hurts."

"They did a good job of turning us around, though. I can't tell you where the entrance is." Outside their cells was a cement-walled hallway. How far it ran in either direction he couldn't tell no matter how hard he pressed his head against the bars to get a better look.

"I just know I can't take much more of this," she said.

Me neither. Any more beatings and the injuries would turn from superficial to running deep.

Riley took a deep breath and exhaled slowly, trying to calm himself down. The men could come at any moment. There was no way to time it.

"Ever thought about what we're going to do if we don't get out of here?" Sophie asked.

"Can't think like that. If you do, they win. That's what they want you to think. They're trying to break you, Sophie. You have to stay strong."

"I'm trying. It's just that . . . it's just that it hurts so much."

You're not alone. "Stay strong, be brave."

"Have you ever been through anything like this before?"

He thought about lying to her, make up some story about being captured and roughed up to give an example of survival, but he couldn't bring himself to do so. "No. I'm sorry."

"Don't be sorry. I'm glad for you. I think this is the part of the war I missed: all those prisoners. Could only imagine how hard it must've been for them and their families, not knowing if you were going to make it out alive." She paused. "Don't have to imagine now."

"Don't give up. We'll get out. We have to."

It felt like it had been around an hour that had passed since they stopped talking. It was then Riley heard the sound of heavy boots on cement coming from down the hallway, the same sound he heard when the two men came to dish out their punishment.

The same two large men appeared before his cell door, their black uniforms doing little to hide their muscular frames. They each had a shaved head and wore a tight-fitting black cap.

One of the men produced a key attached to a retracting cord on his belt and unlocked Riley's cell.

They entered.

Without a word, one of the men rounded behind Riley and grabbed him by the arms, pulling them behind his back. The other man stepped up to him, cracked the knuckles on each hand, then grimaced. A second later, a fist was delivered to Riley's stomach. His whole body lurched forward from the blow, putting pressure on the joints in his arms.

"No! Stop!" Sophie screamed from the next cell.

No, be quiet, Riley thought. *They'll know you're on the edge of cracking.* Before he could open his mouth to tell her to shut it, the man brought his fist across his jaw, forcing his head to snap to the side.

Riley purposefully let out a grunt, hoping the guy would know that it hurt. The man swung in from the other side and sent his head turning in the opposite direction. The taste of blood was on Riley's tongue. He spat it out.

The man punched him in the chest and made him gasp for breath.

"Okay . . . okay . . ." Riley breathed.

The man kicked him in the stomach. Riley doubled over, and tried ignoring the pain in his arms.

"I'll . . . I'll talk. I'll do whatever you say. Just—" The man struck him again, this time in the shoulder. Pain in his arm ignited. "Just no more," he finished.

The man delivering the beating looked past him to his comrade behind. The man must've nodded because he let go. For a second, Riley thought he'd caught a break but the man in front of him kicked Riley's legs out from underneath him. Riley hit the ground. Sophie was whimpering in the next cell.

"Going to have to shut her up," the man behind Riley said.

"In a moment," said the other man.

Riley rolled onto all fours, his head spinning, his stomach feeling like he was trapped on an out-of-control rollercoaster.

Heart racing, he knew his only chance of survival depended on acting on what he had planned. He just hadn't counted on being on the ground when he did. He started to crawl toward the far side of the bed. If he could just get there, he could get—

The man pulled him onto his feet and delivered another blow across his face. On instinct, Riley swung out and caught the man on the jaw. The man's eyes went wild and he kicked Riley in the gut. Riley doubled over. Sophie screeched in the next cell. Riley turned around.

Have to— The man kicked him in the lower back, sending him sprawling forward on the ground while the man's partner looked on. Riley army-crawled to the end of the bed and reached under it. He grabbed the loose metal bed post on the far end and gave it a yank. It came free and the bed teetered on the remaining three posts.

The man came closer. Riley readied himself and grit his teeth. It was now or never. The man reached forward to hoist him up. Riley spun around on his hands and knees and swung the bed post like a baseball bat. It connected square to the man's temple with a thick and hollow clink. The metal scraped along the skin on the follow-through and produced blood. The other guy immediately came in, fists swinging. Riley knocked them away with the post and heard the clunk of metal on bone.

Staggering to his feet, Riley brought the post down on the man's head, cracking the guy's skull and dropping him. The other fellow tackled him to the ground, the post now between Riley's and the man's body. He had to wriggle it free otherwise he'd take maybe two or three more shots to the head and that would be it. Riley clung to the post with one hand, and with his free hand clocked the guy in the ear. The man punched Riley in the throat. Unable to breath, Riley tried to wrestle free the hand holding the post. Quickly, he was able to pull it out but it was to the side. He wiggled and squirmed beneath the man, who was doing all he could to keep Riley still. Riley got his foot in between him and the man's body and kicked out. He sent the man a couple of feet back. The man fell forward, fists swinging. Riley brought the post in from the side and clocked the guy in the head. The man fell over and hit the cement floor with a thump. It was only now that Sophie's screams again filled his ears.

"Riley! Riley!" she shrieked.

"I'm . . . I'm okay," he wheezed, though it was only a half-truth. His face hurt something fierce and his body felt like he'd just got into it with a fully-armored exo.

"Riley! Riley!" She hadn't heard him.

He rolled over onto his side and caught his breath, spat out some blood. He tried his best to talk louder but it was hard to speak above her screaming. "I'm . . . I'm here. It's okay. It's . . . over." He slowly rolled onto all fours, steadied himself, then got to his feet. He limped over to the open cell door and came around to hers. Only when she saw him did she finally stop screaming.

"Riley, I thought . . . I thought . . ." she said.

"It's okay," he said. "I'm okay." He wiped the blood from his face. "I'll live, anyway. Gimme a sec."

He ambled back into his cell and found the key on one of the men's belts. He returned to her cell and unlocked it. When she came out, she fell into his arms. He staggered back a step. Her embrace only made the pain worse . . . but it felt so good to hold her. When she pulled away she looked deep into his eyes and for a second he thought she was going to kiss him. Their eyes locked onto each other's . . . then she looked away, walked past him and saw his handiwork in his cell.

"Should've done that a few days ago," she said quietly.

"Didn't have the bedpost loose yet. Took a chance," he said. He wiped blood from his mouth again. Right now he just wanted to lie down and ride out the pain, but that wasn't an option.

They had to get out of here.

13

STAKE 48

NICK AND GRAYSON were in the prep room with Commander Tiel. Fifteen other soldiers surrounded them. They were discussing their second attempt at infiltrating the hills. Their first . . . too many men wearing exos in the forest. They had been out-gunned.

"We learned last time that those woods are heavily guarded," Tiel said. "This time we'll be ready, unless they've escalated, too. I want you in pairs and to raid those woods like it's your job."

It is, Grayson thought absentmindedly and with a bit of a smirk.

Tiel continued. "Red team will take the west, Blue the east, Green the north. If Riley and Sophie are in there, it'll be up to Fox and Wilder to get them out. Step one is to clear the area. Step two is for Fox and Wilder to lead the Green team into the base while Red and Blue stand guard. If a firefight starts inside, Blue will go in after them. Red remains outside no matter what to take out any escaping the hills. We'll also be bringing in some extra reinforcements. I'll be manning comm. from here. Does everyone understand?"

Several "Yes, sirs," sounded in the room. Others nodded.

"Understood," Grayson said.

"Good. Now let's suit up and move out," Tiel said.

As Nick and Grayson walked with the Green team to the staging area, Nick said, "This took too long."

"It's a second attempt. We needed planning," Grayson said.

"Shouldn't have gone in undermanned in the first place. Seems Tiel was still trying to keep his circle small. What is it about Manta Six that he feels the need to be so secretive?"

"You tell me."

"I know they're a force not to be trifled with. They ran the best op teams during the war. My question is if there's something going on that we don't know about. You have to remember that some of our suits had been stolen, which indicates someone was working on the inside." Then he added as if in afterthought, "I wonder where Tiel's loyalties truly lie?"

"Are you suggesting—"

"Just thinking out loud."

If Nick was hinting at Tiel being a double agent—and she was pretty sure Nick was—then what was about to go down would all be in vain. Was Tiel setting them up for a trap? Was he indeed working with the enemy? He'd given no indication—at least to her—that he was. Aside from the secrecy, there was nothing said or done that would suggest Tiel was allied with Manta Six or the enemy in general.

"What do we do?" she asked.

"Just carry out the orders. It's all we can do. But be mindful, be watchful. If something is up, it'll be sure to present itself eventually. Things don't stay secrets forever."

She hoped he was right.

◆ ◆ ◆

THE HILLS

After finding their way out of the cell block, Sophie and Riley found themselves in a stone corridor.

"They must've built this place during the war," Sophie said.

"The war would've been a good cover," Riley replied. "No one would've batted an eye at seeing equipment around the hills as there was some construction going on amidst all the destruction."

Riley had to pause from walking every twenty or thirty feet. Sophie felt bad for the guy. Should she come up alongside him and offer for him to lean on her shoulder, or would that put him off? He was an independent man and liked to do things on his own. He might think needing to use her as a crutch would be a sign of weakness.

They rounded a bend in the corridor then jumped back a step when they saw a couple of armed soldiers walking toward them.

"What do we do?" she whispered.

"Don't have a choice," he said and nodded for her to move a bit further back the way they'd just came.

She waited with him with their backs against the wall, Riley taking the lead. When the first officer rounded the corner, Riley swung out and did an arm bar across the man's chest. The officer tipped backward, lost his footing, and fell. The second one immediately went for his plasma rifle and aimed it at her. Riley tackled him from the side and took him to the ground. The first officer was getting to his feet. Sophie ran up to him and kicked him in the head, knocking him flat, then followed up by bringing her leg straight up and down with an axe kick to his gut, her heel landing like a hammer onto his solar plexus. She finished him off by kneeling over him and punching him square on the button.

Riley wrestled with the other officer. She could tell by the hard time he was having that his injuries were getting the best of him. She took the fallen officer's plasma rifle and fired a round into the other officer's back, stunning him. The plasma effect would temporarily cripple him. Another blow would kill him. After all the violence they'd endured the past week, she didn't feel like taking a life so she stormed up to the officer and swung the butt of the rifle like a golf club at his head, knocking him out. Riley rolled away, then slowly got to his feet.

"Nice one," he breathed, then coughed.

"Here," she said and reached down and took the other officer's plasma rifle. She handed it to Riley. "Use this."

He took it, looked it over, then readied the weapon. "At least we have some firepower now."

"Just in time, too," she said and nodded toward the end of the corridor. Voices of other officers rose on the air. "How many do you think there are?"

"Sounds like three or four."

They went back along the wall, out of sight.

"The bodies!" she said and bolted forward. She couldn't believe she almost forgot to hide the evidence. "Give me a hand."

She and Riley dragged the unconscious officers around the corner and out of sight. They waited against the wall.

"When they get close, jump out and start firing," she said.

"Good plan."

"It's our only plan." Her heart sped up with each passing moment. She hoped there were *only* three or four enemy officers. Any more and she doubted her and Riley would survive. Her heartbeat drummed thick in her ears as she waited for the officers to approach. When she thought they were close enough, she motioned for Riley to get ready. Slowly, she nodded her head, counting it off. On three, they spun out from around the corner and let them have it. The first shot hit the leading officer square in the chest. The second took out the legs of another. Riley fired off two blasts in rapid succession and took out another one. The final guy had his weapon out and shot in their direction. They dove back behind the corner.

Riley went low; she went high. He quickly fired off a shot at the man's legs, taking them out from underneath him. On instinct, she shot the man in the chest. The guy fell and his body shook as he laid on the ground. The two shots would kill him.

"Oh shoot," she said. She hadn't meant to take a life but had acted in the moment.

"It's okay," he said, "you didn't have a choice."

They rounded the corner and looked at the bodies. One guy groaned. Riley struck him with the butt of his rifle.

"But I did. I just wasn't thinking," she said.

"This is life or death. We live. Someone died. That's the way it goes."

She knew what he meant, but it didn't make her feel any better.

"Let's go," he said, and gave a tug on her arm.

As they ran down the corridor, she asked, "Any idea where we're going?"

"No. Just look for signs or labels or anything that would indicate a way out. If you see a window— whatever—let me know. We'll take what we can get."

She hoped the sound of plasma fire hadn't alerted anyone else.

♦ ♦ ♦

THE FOREST

Nick and Grayson wore green exo-suits and marched with the other armored men through the woods by the hills after flying there. In the lead, Nick kept his cannon ready, knowing they weren't alone in the woods.

This would be a straight-up-take-no-prisoners march. The endgame: get to the foot of the hills and find an entrance.

Nick got on the comm. "All right, fan out a little bit, but stay close enough to keep each other in view. Stay in twos and always get the other guy's back, understood?"

"Yes, sirs," came over his comm.

He was glad Commander Tiel put him in charge of this mission and he liked being in control. Not that he craved the power or status, but as a long-time soldier, he'd seen his fair share of battles and knew how to act. One of the secrets was to keep things as simple as possible.

He had his scanners on and had them set on movement detection. Aside from his comrades around him, so far they were alone. He knew it wouldn't be like that for long.

Grayson marched alongside him. He had to hand it to her, coming out of her shell like this. She was a skilled exo warrior, there was no doubt about that. He'd seen her credentials, but he also got the sense she was something of a peacemaker and liked to avoid violence where she could, which was why she'd previously been assigned surveillance missions as opposed to assaults.

They marched on for a few minutes, cannons always at the ready.

A shot was fired in their direction. Him and Grayson immediately went on the defensive.

Clever. The shot had been fired from far away, thus being out of range from his scanner.

"Get ready," he told Grayson over his comm.

"Always," she replied.

His scanners picked up movement on the west. He hid in behind the thick trunk of a fallen tree and waited. Another shot passed over him just as he ducked down. Grayson dove in behind the criss-crossing branches of two trees that had fallen next to each other.

Weapons fire rose on the air around them as a fleet of enemy exos closed in. His men lit up their cannons and returned fire.

Nick rounded the tree and got in behind an enemy exo rushing by. He amped up the charge on his weapon and let loose and fired straight into the kill switch at the back of this exo's head. The suit collapsed in a heap of metal. He shot off a plasma burst into the suit, ensuring it'd stay down.

He had Grayson pegged on his scanner, but she was out of his visual. No matter. She could take care of herself.

He hoped.

Two more enemy exos came in, sending shot after shot in his direction. Nick returned fire on one, rolled, then blasted the other. They both went down. He had to be careful not to get hit himself.

The sound of heavy plasma fire on the air told him they had just entered an all-out assault phase. His scanner showed fifteen additional exos to his own men. It was clear Manta Six didn't want anyone coming close to the hills. Why now this protection grid after all this time of playing possum, he didn't know. Their sudden zeal in protecting their compound suggested that whatever was going on inside the hill was of grave importance to them and they weren't going to chance anyone standing in their way.

Nick bounded through the woods, keeping one eye on his scanner, the other on his visor for a real-life visual. An enemy exo on the right was quickly taken care of with a plasma burst, while another on the left fired his way. Its shot caught him, its force sending him spinning in a circle. He rounded about and returned fire, hitting the enemy square in the chest. He fired another shot for good measure. The thing went down. More plasma fire headed his way. Some of the bursts came in slow enough he was able to duck and roll and get out of harm's way. Others sent him diving in behind another fallen tree. The tree at his back quickly went up in splinters. He moved forward, diving in behind another.

"There's so many of them," Grayson said through his comm.

"Keep moving. They seem to be having trouble with moving targets. Don't stay in one place too long. You see black, you fire, understand?" he said.

"Got it. Thanks for the tip."

"Don't mention it."

According to his scanner, an enemy exo was behind him, just on the other side of the tree. Nick repositioned himself, leapt over the tree and came crashing down onto it. The enemy landed on its back. He fired a plasma round into the thing's head unit, no doubt scrambling whoever was inside. He delivered a blow with his cannon, smashing the thing's visor, exposing the trembling enemy soldier within.

"How many are you?" Nick said.

The man didn't reply.

"How many!"

The guy only laughed. With a grunt, Nick gently struck the man's face and knocked the guy out.

Bad move.

He should've been more patient and tried to get the information out of him. Then again, with all the heavy fire, he didn't want to be in one place for too long. He got up and surveyed his surroundings. Up ahead of him, one of his men and an enemy exo were exchanging blows like two boxers in the final round. His man prevailed by kicking out and sending the enemy exo back before firing off a plasma round into it. Over to the side and a bit behind him, two other exos plowed into each other like a couple of bulls. His man went down and the enemy exo jumped on top of him. The enemy fired off a shot square into his man's head. Nick bounded over, cannon firing. He dropped the enemy then got down beside his fallen man.

The suit was mangled, but seemed to be intact.

"Are you all right, soldier?" he asked.

It took a moment before he replied, but he groaned, "I'll . . . live."

"Good. Now get up and let's finish this thing."

"Yes, sir."

The man got up and the two fired off rounds into the exos coming toward them. His scanner beeped and he saw more and more enemy exos were entering the fray. He thought of Grayson and wondered how she was fairing.

◆ ◆ ◆

Grayson ran through the woods, dodging around trees and running in between plasma fire. All her combat experience had been in the simulator, but that program was rigged for more one-on-one combat, sometimes two-on-one. It took a while for her reflexes and muscle memory of controlling the suit to kick back in. She seemed to be managing things full swing now, though.

She came up in behind a fallen tree. Its trunk was so thick and wide it was like a wooden wall before her. According to her scanner, there was an enemy exo on the other side of it. After all the heavy fire, her plasma levels were running low. She had to conserve. Slowly, she walked up to the tree, doing her best not to make a sound. Once right up to it, she activated her thrusters, rose above it, then came crashing down on the enemy. The exo unit collapsed beneath her when she landed on it. She hit her thrusters again, rose up, then dropped down on it again, smashing it. She came down on it one more time with the heavy foot of her suit, crushing its cannon arm.

Plasma fire ripped past her and sent the tree up in splinters.

"Oh shoot!" she said and hit the thrusters again and went over it. She landed on the other side and readied her cannon. She hadn't been paying attention and hadn't seen the enemy exo on her scanner. The thing was just on the other side of the tree. Another one was coming in from off to the side. A moment later, it was in visual range through her visor.

She fired, sending a plasma burst into the one on the side. Quickly, she rounded about the tree, hoping to surprise the one that had originally fired at her. It worked and she sent a round into it. The shot failed to hit square on, only struck the thing's left leg. She started running through the woods, trying to get as far away from it as possible. A moment later she came upon the fallen green exo-suit of one of her men. It lay there, covered in black burn marks.

"Are you al—" Before she could finish the question, plasma fire rained around her. She had no choice but to kick on the thrusters and fly straight up, hopefully out of range.

◆ ◆ ◆

Nick came across a red exo duking it out with a black one. He offered assistance by coming in from the rear, grabbing hold of the black exo's head unit, then giving a twist, warping the metal. Sparks flew, and the black exo turned around. With a single blast, it shot Nick point blank, sending him flying back.

He landed with a grunt. About to fire a second shot at him, the black exo was quickly taken out by the red one.

Nick got up. "Thanks, soldier."

"My honor, sir," the red exo said.

The two quickly stood back-to-back as black exos dropped from the trees. Nick and the red exo let loose with everything they had and took the black ones out.

Can't take another hit, Nick thought.

The red exo fired a shot into the trees then activated its thrusters and flew off.

And now I'm alone. Supposed to stay in twos. So much for that idea.

He checked his scanner. There were still more enemies. "Going to have to bring in the heavy artillery soon," he said to himself. As for his own suit, another plasma burst in the right spot would keep him down. He couldn't risk it so he did the only thing he could think of: fly upward.

Hoping to use the ground-focused battle to his advantage, he decided to take to the trees. Now, perched twenty feet above the battle ground, he stood on an enormous tree limb and checked his scanner. Two enemy exos were coming in on the north. Readying his cannon like a sniper, he fired off two successive shots, temporarily stunning them. He quickly left his perch, not wanting them to retrace the trajectory, and landed on another gigantic branch, this one some thirty or so feet up from the battlefield. He fired off a few more shots, pegging the unsuspecting exos below.

Should've done this from the start, he thought.

Nick moved to another branch, this one lower. He took down another enemy exo from behind.

His scanner beeped and an enemy exo was coming in for him hard and fast. He spun around and shot it down out of the air. The thing crashed to the ground. Nick hit the thrusters and flew to a fallen tree trunk. He fired off a few more rounds then had to stop when a half dozen enemy exos all closed in on him at once.

Grayson landed east of the battlefield and watched as blue exos clashed with black ones. A couple were locked in a wrestling match, while others sent shots from in behind fallen trees. She tried to help them out as best she could and fired on every black exo she set her eyes on.

One to the right fired at her. She took the blow and rolled with it. It had just skimmed her and didn't do any severe damage. She returned fire—two shots—and took the enemy down. Another one was at the north. She fired at it and dropped it. She knew that the single shots only momentarily slowed them down. There hadn't been explicit orders to kill, just to attack. She hated the idea of taking a life and hoped that even if she completely destroyed an exo, the pilot would still survive. Without their suits, they were powerless in this kind of fight anyway so the only thing they could do would be either stay in the suit for their protection or chance it and get out of it and try and stay alive amidst all the plasma fire.

Blue and black exos exchanged fire back and forth. Some of the blues went down. Then some of the black ones. She knew she had to get back to Nick and maintain their dual formation.

She got on the comm. "Fox, do you read me?"

"Loud and clear, Wilder. I have you out of range on my scanner. Where are you?"

"East. Don't ask. Need to get back to you."

"Roger. I suggest making your way here. I'd come there but you're supposed to be with your battalion."

"Can you meet me part way?"

"Kind of got a sticky situation here. I could really use the backup."

"Copy. I'm on my way." Grayson fired and took out a black exo coming toward her. She turned on her thrusters and headed into the sky. She had only been traveling about ten seconds when a plasma burst came toward her from the ground and sent her spiraling.

14

THE SKY

Grayson's world went upside down then right side up, over and over again. She hit the stabilizers and righted herself. A black exo was in hot pursuit, presumably the one that sent her spiraling. She opened fire on it, giving it all she had. The black exo maneuvered around the streaks of plasma fire until one hit it in the chest and sent it tumbling backward. Grayson fired again and zapped the thing in the head. She fired once more and sent it crashing to the ground.

Quickly, she adjusted her flight path and headed toward Nick.

◆ ◆ ◆

THE HILLS

Riley and Sophie raced through the stone corridors, searching for a way out. Unfortunately, there were no exit signs nor were there any internal maps indicating where one was inside this labyrinth.

They had taken out a few more guards and spent the last half hour hiding in a broom closet while they waited for a few enemy officers to clear the corridor.

"Let's face it," Sophie said, "we're lost."

"We're not lost," Riley said. "Just . . . misplaced."

"As if. And it's not like we can stop and ask for directions."

"Now why didn't I think of that?" he said. They'd been too busy defending themselves that Riley kicked himself in the pants for not interrogating at least one of the officers they dropped for a way out. He'd ask the next one.

The two moved quietly through what had to be the umpteenth corridor, rifles armed and ready.

◆ ◆ ◆

THE FOREST

Nick was surrounded. Six black exos all had their cannons trained on him. Even if he could take out two of them, that still left four to contend with. He'd go down, especially with having already taken a plasma hit. So he did the only thing he could do—

He put his hands up.

One of the black exos moved in.

"Identify yourself," came the voice through the speaker. "Name and unit."

Nick tapped on his own visor then raised his hands, feigning his communicator was broken.

"I said name and unit!"

He repeated the gesture. There was no way he was going to give up that information.

The exo pressed his cannon up to him. "Step out of the suit. You're coming with us."

He thought he should pretend he didn't hear him, but that wouldn't work because he just responded to his demand for his name.

Should he fight? It was either risk death or be captured.

He spotted an incoming exo on his scanner. Grayson? If he could just buy a little more time.

"I said get out of the suit, hands on your head!" The guy inside the black exo was clearly ticked.

Nick put his hands down as slowly as possible, making every long second count. Discreetly, he armed the tasers built into the exo's hands. If the guy tried to touch him, the enemy suit would be fried.

The exo on his scanner was closing in. Please be Grayson or, at least, a friendly.

A barrage of plasma fire rained down from the sky, knocking down two of the enemy exos. Nick lunged forward and gripped the one in front of him, sending a shockwave of electricity through the black exo's systems. He rolled off him and fired at another one. More plasma fire came down as a green exo landed beside him and laid waste to the two remaining exos.

Nick finished them off with blasts from his cannon, then came over to another that lay on the ground and sent electricity through it.

When he righted himself, he turned to the exo that rescued him. "Wilder?"

"In the flesh. Sort of."

"Thank you."

"No problem. Looked like you were going to be a goner, there."

"Felt like it, too. You came just in time."

"Wasn't as far out as I thought."

The two sent a couple more plasma bursts into the fallen exos, ensuring they would stay down.

"Was over by Blue team," she said. "They seem to be holding up, but I don't know for how long."

"Seems that way with the Reds, too."

The two started to head back toward the Hills.

More exos entered the scanner's range and Nick's heart sank. "They're not letting up. They're clearly protecting something."

"They're protecting their base."

"Yeah, but what's inside it that's so important? This doesn't seem to just be about protecting their headquarters."

Low thuds shook the ground. Nick knew that vibration even in his exo-suit.

"Looks like the cavalry's arrived," he said. "Let's take a look."

Him and Grayson activated their thrusters and rose above the forest. Below, the flashing lights of plasma fire from both sides lit up the landscape like lights on a Christmas tree. In front of them, making their way through the forest and stepping on the already-fallen trees, were three-story tall mech-bots.

Gambits. There were two of them.

"Took Tiel long enough," Grayson said.

"He wanted to make sure we needed them."

♦ ♦ ♦

THE HILLS

Sophie moved ahead of Riley as they ebbed down yet another corridor. She came to a corner, stopped, then slowly peered to both sides, rifle at the ready.

"Clear," she said, and turned right.

"Could be the other way," he said.

"Or it could be this way."

"They no doubt know we're on the run. We need to find a way out and fast."

"Tell me something I don't know."

They came to the end of this corridor and found a flight of metal stairs. They led up.

"Most likely we're still below ground," she said. "Let's go."

They cautiously went up the stairs, doing their best for their steel-toed boots to not make any noise when walking on it. Riley still moved slowly. His injuries would have to be tended to once they made their way back to base. Not that she was faring any better; she was sore all over and bruised in places she never thought would be hurt in a million years, but at least she could walk without trouble.

At the top of the stairs was a door. She signaled for Riley to open it while she took aim. He pulled on the door handle and yanked it open. She aimed her rifle to both sides. A lone officer was walking toward them. She sent a plasma burst into his chest and dropped him.

They entered the hallway. This one was finished, no stone walls. They were concrete, with an assortment of heavy metal doors running off of it. The doors also had signage. Some were maintenance closets, a couple were bathrooms. Another two appeared to be offices.

Voices rose on the air and they started to jog forward. Whoever was coming would see the body of the guy she just shot. Soon this hallway would be swarming with officers. They went down the hall and saw a sign with a red equilateral cross.

The infirmary.

More voices rose on the air as did the footfalls of boots.

They entered the room and closed the door.

A man in a light blue medical uniform shouted, "Hey, what are you doing here!" He immediately ran for a comm. unit on the wall.

Sophie fired and shot the unit.

A man lying in a nearby bed gave a shout as someone who appeared to be a nurse came running into the room. The nurse wore a pair of scrubs.

Riley had his weapon raised at who Sophie assumed was the doctor. "How many of you are in here?"

The doctor raised his hands. "F-five. Myself, my nurse, and three patients. Please, we don't want any trouble."

You were about to start some by going for the comm., Sophie thought. She kept her weapon trained on the nurse while Riley had his on the doctor.

The patients squirmed in their beds, but they weren't any threat. They seemed either too sick or too injured to be much to worry about.

"What's the fastest way out?" Riley demanded.

"Outside?" the doctor said.

"Yes, outside. How do I get there?"

"And why should I help you?"

Riley fired past him and blew up the I.V. unit connected to one of the patients. The patient screamed.

The doctor kept his hands raised. "Okay, okay, take it easy. You need to go out this door, head to the end of the hallway, and take the staircase up two levels. Once at the top, you need to turn le—"

"Help! Somebody help!" It came from the far side of the room. One of the patients had hobbled over to the second comm. unit and was shouting into it.

"Stop it!" Sophie said, weapon pointed at him.

"Not a chance." The patient started coming toward her. He was unarmed.

"Get back in bed."

He kept coming.

"I mean it. Don't make me shoot you."

The man was almost up to her and raised his fist.

"I'm serious!"

He swung at her. She fired. The man went flying back and skidded along the floor. She hadn't meant to shoot, but instinct had taken over.

One of the patients let out a yelp and stared at her panic-stricken, tears and all.

"No more," the doctor said.

"Repeat it," Riley told him. "Tell me the way out."

"End of the hallway. A staircase. Go two floors up and—"

The door crashed open and two officers entered, weapons drawn. "Put the rifles down!" one of them shouted.

Riley spun around and shot one, then dove for cover behind a heart monitor. The other officer fired at Sophie the same time she fired at him. Their plasma bursts crossed paths. They both missed. Sophie went behind a wall at the far side of the room. Another shot went out and someone yelled. She peeked around the corner and saw the doctor had gone down. Riley fired at the officer and struck him. A third officer came into the room, weapon blazing. His shot took out the nurse. Riley fired back and killed him with a shot to the head.

She waited by the wall, weapon ready, in case any more would come. After five minutes, she came out.

Riley had his rifle against a patient's head. "The way out!"

The guy seemed so hopped up on medication he couldn't form any words. Riley stormed over to the last patient.

"Dead," he said. "Didn't get hit. Heart attack?"

"I don't know," she said, "but we need to get out of here."

"Staircase at the end of the hallway. Two floors up. Turn left, I think."

"Then let's go."

They exited the room and made their way to the staircase. That doctor better have been right.

♦ ♦ ♦

THE FOREST

Grayson had to admit her heart rose with relief at the sight of the towering mech-bots. Each walked on two legs as wide as a car, their bodies cockpits like those of a jet. Each had arms as long as tree trunks and three times as wide. Weaponry protruded from the sides of the arms, which ended in clenched fists. She wasn't sure how adept they were at finger work. As they made their way through the forest, the giant fallen trees were further splintered beneath them.

Let's see the enemy go up against those! she thought.

Quickly, the armory at the side of the arms lit up and began firing rapid bursts of heated light rays. It was a relatively new technology. By concentrating beams of light, they were able to harness the created heat and focus them with near laser precision.

Black exos ran through the forest, opening plasma fire at the enormous mechs. Their shots simply were absorbed by the mechs' hulls. A few left a couple of burn marks, but nothing serious.

As the black enemy exos appeared out of the forest like bees escaping a hive, trying to take the mechs down, Grayson saw it as open season and fired. She pegged two up ahead of her, then moved quickly to take another one from behind. Some returned fire so she sped up her gait and maneuvered out of the way.

A few enemy exos ignited their thrusters and flew up onto the hull of the mech-bot. On top, they began firing plasma and bullets into the shielding around the cockpit. Grayson boosted her own thrusters and rose up off the forest floor, getting even in height with the exos on top of the mech. Like picking cans off a fence post with a BB gun, she sent burst after burst into the exos on top of the mech, cleaning them off. The mech's mechanical arms whirred and it changed tactics. Gatling guns flipped out from the sides and it sprayed the surrounding forest in a barrage of bullets. Grayson was thankful she was in the air and in the clear. She searched the ground for Nick. He was well off to the side, trading blows with another enemy exo. Grayson flew over to him and together they took the enemy exo down.

She glanced up and saw the two giant mechs had parted ways and one was heading closer to the hills. Knowing it'd be greeted by a fleet of enemy exos, she flew after it. Grayson realized there wasn't much she could do solely on her own to help out the giant bot, but figured if she could keep a few enemy exos off of it, it'd be at least some help.

She kept up her flight in behind it, then quickly remembered they were supposed to stay in pairs. She got on the comm. "Nick, do you copy?"

"Read you loud and clear."

"I'm following the second bot closer to the hills. It's going to be greeted with heavy fire, no doubt. I suggest you come with me."

"Be right there."

"Also suggest radioing in the other units so we can come up on the hills en masse."

"Good idea. I'll make the necessary notifications."

"Copy. See you soon."

"Fox, out."

Grayson fired from the sky, striking enemy exos where she could. Many of them changed their trajectory and began going after the giant mech.

She took out two more and her plasma level indicator beeped. She was out of juice. Quickly, she loaded up the half-dozen—mini rockets the size of eggs, a smaller version of the tech on the mech-bots—and heard the motors whir on her shoulders as things got ready to fire. Landing just behind the mech, she waited until a half dozen enemy exos emerged out of the woodwork then let them have it. The mini rockets connected squarely with their targets and went off, taking the suits down. She loaded up her mini Gatlings around her wrists then bounded over to the fallen exos and fired several bullets into each suit, hoping at least one would pierce the armor and scramble a circuit or two. She got one, then went over to another that had fallen over on its side. With precise aim, she fired several bullets into the kill switch section of the back of the head unit. Sparks flew and she knew she hit paydirt. Grayson went over to another fallen exo and did the same.

Plasma fire struck her from behind, knocking her forward. She hit the ground, rolled, stood, then fired up her thrusters and ascended into the sky, not looking back. Below, the mech she'd been following was cleaning house, taking down exos and making quick work of annihilating them. Just then she saw a couple of black exos bounding away from the mech's feet. A moment later, a violent explosion lit up around the mech's foot units. Shrapnel and debris burst outward. The mech teetered then fell forward, the cockpit slamming into the ground like the head of a hammer.

"The pilot!" Grayson said. She flew down and landed near the cockpit. She grabbed onto the seam and, using her exo's enhanced strength, pulled, trying to pry it open. Its front was so lodged into the ground that she was working against the earth clamped against it.

"Stay back!" she shouted through the speaker, hoping the pilot inside heard her. She readied her laser cannon then opened fire at the cockpit, focusing the beam near the seam, the aim being to cut out a small hole for the pilot to crawl out of.

An enemy exo flew in from the side and crashed into her. The two rolled along the ground. It aimed its cannon at her. She let the laser loose on it and sliced off its arm, then readjusted her aim and sliced along the head unit. Only when the head rolled off the exo-suit and exposed the decapitated man inside did she realize what she'd done.

"Oh no, I'm sorry. I'm so sorry," she said and fought back the tears. *Come on, get it together. You can cry later.* Somehow, ending a life in such a manner ate at her.

Blinking back more tears, she went back to the cockpit and opened laser fire against it. Focusing the beam and holding it in one spot, it slowly burned its way through the hull and she began to cut an opening about one foot by two. When she finished, she reached in and pried the makeshift lid away and threw it to the side. Inside, the pilot was crouched on the far side of the cockpit. Thankfully, she hadn't struck him with the laser.

"Now you can get out, but stay here for now for your own protection. Are you armed?" she asked.

The pilot, a young man, nodded. "Thank you."

"You're welcome."

An enemy exo bounded in from the side. An explosion sounded not too far away. Just as the enemy exo locked its weapon on her, Nick flew in and opened fire, taking it down. Once it fell, he came up to it and smashed down on it with his cannon. The cannons were built like battering rams, meant for long- and close-range combat. Sparks flew and the enemy was down.

"Just in the nick of time," she said then realized that sounded kind of corny given his name.

She didn't think he noticed because he said, "Are you all right?"

"I'll live. The pilot of this mech-bot's okay, too."

"The one back there is making quick work of those coming up to it."

"We should tell it to mind its feet. That's how this one was taken down."

"Noted." Nick went silent for a moment and she assumed he had gotten on another channel, notifying the pilot of the other mech to keep an eye out.

"We still closing in on the hills?" she asked.

"Keep moving forward," he said. "We stay together from here on out, though, if it can be helped."

"Good plan."

"You've done well, soldier."

"Thanks."

"But this battle's not over yet." His words were firm and any hint of a compliment was gone from his voice.

"I know. Things are getting crazy. I wonder what they're protecting?"

♦ ♦ ♦

Riley and Sophie followed the doctor's orders and went up the stairs and took the appropriate turns. So far, it seemed the doctor's advice was right on the money as up here was where all the action was. They had managed to avoid personnel in the hallways by hiding between door posts or slipping into a side room while they waited for those roaming the halls to pass.

They stood inside the doorframe to another stairwell.

"Too bad there aren't any exit signs," Sophie said.

"Could be a security precaution," Riley said, "specifically for people like us."

"Doc didn't say where we should go after this."

"Looks like we're on our own again."

"I'm getting used to it." She offered him a playful wink.

Even now, with her forehead shiny, her ponytail loose, and strands of stray hair covered in sweat, she was beautiful.

Maybe when this was over he could talk to her. He felt a little silly for even thinking it, but a part of him wondered if this experience would somehow draw them closer together.

"How's your charge on that thing?" he asked, nodding toward her rifle.

"About fifty percent. Yours?"

"Sixty."

"Guess I'm a little more trigger-happy than you."

"Or they weren't charged equally when we got 'em."

"Always an answer for everything."

Voices rose on the air as did a multitude of footfalls.

Sophie's eyes went wide.

"Let's go," he whispered, and the two headed down the hallway.

From behind, "You there!"

Riley glanced over his shoulder and saw a handful of officers coming toward them. They aimed their rifles and started firing. Riley and Sophie ran in a zig zag pattern, making themselves harder to shoot at, the heat from the plasma soaring by them a reminder of how lucky they were.

They rounded a corner. Riley had his back against the wall and stuck out his rifle. He fired off several shots, working blind. Even if the shots didn't hit the officers, at least they'd force them to slow down until the fire abated. Sophie crouched down by his legs and peeked around the corner. The moment she stuck her head out, shots were fired her way. She jolted back.

"They're coming," she said.

Riley searched the hallway. There were three sets of double doors. One straight ahead, and two staggered to either side.

"Let's go," he said, and they ran down the hallway. "In here." They went to the door on the left and found themselves on a grated catwalk. There was a window looking out into the hallway they'd just came from so they crouched down and duck-walked beneath the sill, staying out of sight. The catwalk ran the length of the room and there was a stairway at the end. It led down into a small room with a security door with a swipe card mechanism next to it. They were trapped.

"I have an idea," he whispered. "Go down the stairs and get underneath this thing. I'll join you in a second."

"You sure?" she asked.

"Yeah. They're going to search here anyway if they don't come in here first. We need to take them down."

"Okay," she said and moved to the end of the catwalk.

Taking a deep breath then exhaling slowly, Riley went back to the door they just came through. He opened the door and looked out. The officers were moving down the hallway. He fired off a shot and got their attention.

"There!" one of them shouted.

Riley slammed the door and ran to the end of the catwalk, took the stairs down two at a time, then rounded back in under the catwalk where Sophie waited.

"Ready?" he said.

She nodded, and the two aimed their weapons upward.

The door above burst open and the officers started to file in. Some moved quickly, others with caution.

Riley opened fire, sending plasma through the grates in the catwalk, getting the officers from underneath. Sophie moved a little bit ahead of him to cover more range and opened fire herself.

The officers started to drop. One grabbed his radio and shouted into it, "Seven-one, seven-one, Level Two. They're on Level Two near—" Riley shut him up with a shot to his thighs. The man dropped.

"More will be coming," Sophie said.

Riley eyed the room. There was no way out save the way they got in here, unless—

He ran to the catwalk's stairs, went up them, then patted down the security guards. Grabbing one of the officer's clearance cards, he went back along the catwalk and down the stairs.

"Hope this works," he said.

He tried it on the door. The thing beeped and a red light lit up. He tugged on the door. It didn't open.

"Shoot!" he said. He looked over his shoulder. Sophie was up by the officers, checking them over. One started to move. She pummeled him with her fist three times in the head and he clocked out. She ran back along the catwalk, took the stairs and came up to Riley.

"Here, try one of these," she said and fanned out three cards for him to choose from.

He took them and one by one tried them on the door. It was the final card that did it and the light by the door lit up green.

"You're beautiful, thank you," he said and kissed her forehead. He hadn't meant to, but did it without thinking.

He heard her say a soft, "Oh," before coming up behind him as they went through the door.

They were in a small hallway, this one only some twenty feet long. Another door was at the end. They went up to it and Riley noticed the camera in the corner at the far end.

"Don't look up," he said.

"Why?"

And he knew she looked up.

"That's not good," she said.

"Just keep moving."

He tried the same swipe card that got them into this hallway at the mechanism by the door. It worked. The light went green. Riley opened the door then held it open a few inches with his foot. Without entering, he peered in. The coast was clear.

"Okay, let's go," he said.

When they got through, they were behind a wall of metal crates along with some wooden ones. The ceiling was extremely high, metal with rafters. Were they on ground level because this looked like a hangar?

The lighting was dim.

"Careful," he told her and the two crept along behind the wooden crates. He kept his eyes peeled for a door.

An office was on his left, then more crates. They moved to the far end of the room. They rounded the crates to see what was on the other side.

His heart began to gallop.

15

THE HANGAR

Riley stood in shock. Before him was a fleet of exo soldiers. There must've been three hundred of them all lined up in formation. He didn't think the suits were empty either as what appeared to be senior officers were peppered throughout the ranks, stepping up to each soldier and exchanging a few words.

Ahead of the fleet were three mech-bots on each side, each at least four stories tall, all on two wide mechanical legs. The cockpits were rounded, with a cannon mounted on top of each. Their arms each held a single rocket, ready for direct-aim firing.

In front of them all was an enormous, gleaming silver sphere with metal plates covering it. The sphere had to be at least a hundred feet in diameter. On either side of the sphere were giant black metal arches.

People who appeared to be scientists in lab coats worked a vast array of equipment in front of the sphere, many others behind multiple screens and monitors off to each side.

In front of the sphere some thirty feet away from it was what looked like a giant cannon mounted on a huge black tripod.

Sophie came up beside him. "Oh my . . ." she said when she saw it.

"Something big's happening," Riley said. "But look at them. They're all lined up, but there's nothing but a wall behind that metal circle thing."

"Maybe there's huge hangar doors but we just can't see them from here?"

"Looks like they're preparing an all-out assault."

"On who? The city?"

"I don't know." He checked back the way they'd just come from and so far no one had followed them. "We can't stay here."

"If we go back, we'll be arrested again."

Suddenly his injuries didn't feel so bad. Adrenaline?

"I just don't know what we're going to do," he said.

◆ ◆ ◆

THE HILLS

They were at the foot of the hills now. From what Nick could see, there were no visible openings. Obviously the door in was hidden.

He took out a black exo that had tried to get the drop on him and Grayson from behind with a few quick plasma bursts.

The giant mech-bot behind him was taking care of some more.

Red and Blue team members began to gather around him. He noticed their numbers were few, as were the other Green team members that joined them.

"I think we're going to have to blow it open," he told Grayson. He got on the comm. "This is Nick Fox for Commander Tiel."

"Copy, Fox. I see through your visual you've made it. Good job."

"We can't find a way in, sir."

"There has to be one. Send a team forward to examine the rocks and see what they find."

"And if they don't find anything?"

"We'll cross that bridge when we get there."

"Understood." To Grayson, "We move in and survey." He got on all channels. "I want two lineups at the base of the hills, one facing out, the other facing in. Anyone who doesn't belong to us gets taken down. Green team, I want two more with me, Hendricks and Johnson. We scan and search the rocks for any sign of an opening. Report your findings to me."

"Yes, sirs," came over the comm.

"Let's go, Wilder," he said, and he and Grayson approached the rocks, scanners on.

◆ ◆ ◆

THE HANGAR

All they could do was lay low and not give away their position. Riley and Sophie stayed hunkered down in the corner. Now and then Riley rose and surveyed the room, searching for an exit. There was a wide door off to the side, presumably where they brought in the exo-armored soldiers. The mechs would've had to have been built in here—or at least pieced together—because he couldn't see any other doors. He could be wrong, however. The lighting in here was dim, with only a few overhead. The main lights were by the computers and where the scientists worked around that giant gun thing.

Were they crafting a weapon? Was it here they were using the particle accelerator for something? He should've had Tiel give him the specs or at least showed him what it looked like. He didn't know if it was an error on Tiel's part or on his for not asking.

He got back down beside Sophie. "We need to make our way over to the far side. There's a large door there."

"Any signs indicating where it leads?"

"Can't see from here. It seems to be our only hope."

◆ ◆ ◆

THE HILLS

Nick, Grayson, Hendricks and Johnson scanned the rock face, searching for an opening. The boulders were piled around each other, some as tall as Nick's exo-suit, others smaller. There weren't any rocks less than the size of an armchair. He checked the crevasses and looked in the cracks where he could.

Nothing.

But it had to open up somehow, whether a big door or small.

Nick had let a few more soldiers help out with the search so a couple of guys had flown up to the top of the hills and were surveying there. A few others were far to the left and right, seeing what they could find.

"Any luck?" Grayson came in through his comm.

"None so far." He glanced down to where she stood a hundred yards away amidst some of the other troops. The men had taken their line formations and stood at the ready. A few plasma bursts went off when black exos appeared out of the woods on the attack. "Can't spend all day up here."

"There has to be a way in."

"There is, and we'll find it." He flew up higher on the rock face and looked it over. Nothing here that would indicate an opening and his scanners read only authentic rocks, nothing fake.

He turned on his heat detector and instructed the other soldiers examining the rocks to do the same.

His visual filled with blue and green. Some yellow registered thanks to the rocks reflecting the heat of the sun. There was a bit of orange, too. No red. Clever. Any heat that might be escaping the opening would be masked by the heat from the rocks.

Manta Six got their act together on this one, he thought.

He kept checking.

◆ ◆ ◆

THE HANGAR

Inside, Riley and Sophie couldn't get a clear pathway to the other side of the room. If they simply went back the way they came behind the crates, they'd hit a wall. At the far end, the crates were stacked four high, all flush together. There was no way to climb them.

"All we can do is bide our time," Riley whispered.

The scientists worked, several huddled around that gun thing. A few of them worked the controls on it, a couple others tapped buttons on the surrounding computers, looked at their data pads, then tapped some more buttons.

"Just be patient," he told her.

All they could do was wait.

◆ ◆ ◆

THE HILLS

Outside, Nick was about to give up then thought to activate his electro-scanner. It detected any electronics in the area. Immediately part of the screen on his visor filled with the surrounding exos. He had to narrow the field and just focus it to where he was on the rock face. He tapped a few buttons inside the arm unit and the screen changed. It wasn't picking up anything.

He walked along a rocky ledge, keeping himself facing the rock so the scanner would pick up something.

Soon, the thing beeped.

"Finally," he said.

He hopped up on another boulder then climbed another. About fifteen feet from where he just was he noticed a giant rock partly protruding from the others. He walked alongside it and the signal grew stronger. He kept walking and the signal faded a little. He stepped backward several feet and the signal was strong again.

Nick analyzed the rock and deep within the crevasse where it met another he saw metal. He followed its path and saw that—from his perspective—the tiny metal track went all the way down to the ground, then ran up around ten feet above him.

He moved forward, the signal faded, then it grew strong again.

The other side, he thought. Sure enough, a simple metal band was between another rock and the main rock face.

"Must be a hatched door," he said to himself. He reached for it and tried using the strength of the suit against it. The rock wouldn't budge. He tried again, setting the suit's strength capability to maximum. Instead, chunks of rock broke away in his hands. "Worth a shot." He got on the comm. "Bring in the Gambit. We're blowing this baby open."

◆ ◆ ◆

THE HANGAR

Sophie's ears perked up when she heard the sound of a door opening.

"Riley," she whispered.

The two stood. She heard footfalls. Slowly, they got in behind a crate and peered down the aisle they took to enter this room. An armed officer was coming toward them.

"Here, hide," Riley said and climbed up onto the crate. He dropped down on the other side, getting in between it and another one.

She quickly climbed up and did the same. She dropped down into the shadows. The footfalls grew closer and closer, then moved past them. From what she could hear, the officer rounded the crate from where they just were and proceeded into the open area of the room.

"That was close," she said.

"He might've been a scout looking for us. Hope there aren't any more."

"Me, too."

◆ ◆ ◆

THE HILLS

Nick got back down to ground level and, after instructing the Gambit where to go, came up beside it. The giant arms of the mech-bot seemed to change form as metal compartments opened up along its sleeves and rocket launchers folded out.

"I sent you the read-out," Nick said to the pilot, "now line it up and create an opening."

"Copy."

The giant machine whirred as the metal arms realigned themselves to the proper height and angle.

"Counting down," came the pilot's voice. "On my mark: three, two, one. Mark."

A rocket fired up on one of the arms and a moment later it was away and sped into the rock. In a giant blast that echoed on the air, rocky debris and dust exploded outward from the impact. It blew a hole clean through.

As the dust began to settle, a giant dark rocky corridor was revealed. Soon, rapid fire came blazing out of it as a fleet of black exos emerged from the darkness and let loose with all they had.

"Return fire!" Nick shouted.

The pilot readied the next rocket. "Counting down. Three, two, one. Mark."

The second rocket streamed into the tunnel. A second later, a fireball blasted out of the hole, sending the exos coming out of it up in flames.

Nick aimed his cannon and took out a black exo that escaped. Plasma fire sounded around him as some of the exos still kept coming forward, their suits flameproof.

He bounded up the rock and got into the thick of it, firing shot after shot into the enemy. Several fell. One nicked him. He dropped down, spun around, and returned fire.

His men closed in from the sides and opened fire.

"Wilder, you with me?" Nick shouted through the comm.

"Yes, sir, be right there," she said.

He saw her climbing up the hill. She dropped an exo coming toward her. She shot down another that had made it all the way to the ground. It wasn't long before she was at his side.

"Green team," Nick said into the comm., "follow me in. Red and Blue, finish up out here then I want Blue coming in as well. Red team, remain out here and make sure nothing comes out."

"Yes, sir," many said.

Nick and Grayson entered.

16

RED LIGHTS BEGAN to flash accompanied by a siren. Something was up.

"What's going on?" Sophie asked.

"Don't know." Riley peered over the crate they were behind. The room started to go into a frenzy.

A voice came over the intercom. "Stay in formation. Repeat, stay in formation."

The officers in the room began scurrying about, making their way toward the crates. The scientists began working all the more frantically.

Riley dropped down when more officers came near the crates. From the sounds of things, they moved past them and went back down the aisle behind the crates. He heard a door open and assumed a lot of them filed out. Some remained behind.

His heart picking up speed for fear of getting caught, he got the plasma rifle ready.

"Any second now," he told Sophie.

She nodded, clearly knowing what he meant.

One officer came up to the crate and put something down on it, maybe his weapon. Riley waited, his back to the crate, and listened closely. He couldn't hear anything amidst the shouts and clamoring of footfalls. He waited some more.

Silence.

He closed his eyes and counted back from ten in an effort to calm himself. When he opened them, he got the sense he was being watched. He looked up, only to see the officer standing on the crate, looking down at him, weapon trained.

"Slowly," the officer said. "Drop it."

Riley cautiously got up, nodded at the officer, then went to put his weapon down. He glanced at Sophie. She already had her rifle at her feet.

There'd be no surviving this.

Riley bent low with his weapon, then quickly righted himself and fired, blowing the officer backward off the crate.

A loud whir filled the air. Riley hopped up onto the crate and opened fire at a couple of the officers coming toward it.

"I'm going to die," he said quietly to himself, then shouted, "Get up here!"

He heard Sophie scramble between the crates below, then she climbed up beside him, weapon drawn. She fired at the nearest approaching officer.

Across from them, some from the lines of exos looked at them.

Just when Riley thought they were going to fire and shoot him down, the voice came over the intercom again. "Maintain formation. This facility is under attack. Repeat, maintain formation and proceed as planned."

The giant gun thing lit up bright blue in the metal seams along its shaft and a beam of blue electric light shot forth from it, striking the metallic sphere. The whole room lit up and all eyes were trained on the sphere. As the beam flowed into it, it began to turn and spin, the speed getting faster and faster.

"What in the world . . ." Sophie drawled out.

Riley kept an eye on the guards. Everyone was looking at the sphere.

The sphere spun until all its components were a blur of smooth silver. Was it his imagination or was the silver beginning to melt? It hadn't turned red, but simply began to liquefy and radiate outward like a water droplet bursting in slow motion.

The beam kept pummeling light into the sphere. The two black arms on either side of it lit up, bright blue light emanating between the cracks in the metal plating.

Slowly, a wall of blue light began to form and the sphere slowly melted away from view.

◆ ◆ ◆

THE HILLS

Grayson and Nick led the Green team through the corridor. Unarmored enemy officers appeared and opened fire. They were no match for the exo-suits and were quickly blasted away.

"Which way?" she asked Nick.

"Right," he said and it took her a second to realize that was his response, not an acknowledgment of the question.

They moved through the corridor, firing at any officer that stood in their way. Red lights flashed and a siren sounded.

"All available personnel to the hangar. All available personnel to the hangar," came the voice over the intercom.

Some of the officers coming toward them turned tail and started heading the other way.

"After them," Nick said.

Grayson aimed to chase them down.

THE HANGAR

Sheets of white light radiated outward from the center of the wall of blue light, then collapsed back inward, over and over again.

Riley took the opportunity and nudged Sophie. When she looked at him, he pointed to the two officers just off to the side. She nodded. They crept across the crate, dropped down and fired, taking the officers down.

"Run!" he said and they sprinted the other way. "The door's over here!" He kept one eye looking ahead, the other at the wall of light. They ran in behind the exos. Suddenly the room exploded with the sound of heavy footfalls as the six mechs made their way toward the wall of light.

Riley couldn't help but look. The mech-bots, first one then the others, stepped into the wall of light and disappeared.

His mouth dropped open.

The exo troop went mobile and started their march forward, funneling into the wall of light.

A couple at the rear turned toward them and opened fire.

Riley shot back and he and Sophie ran, dodging the blasts coming their way. They had to round to the side. One of the black exos took out one of his own as Riley ran in between them. It was crazy, but it was the only direction he could turn.

He glanced over his shoulder to make sure Sophie was right behind him. She was.

He fired back, which got the other exos into a frenzy.

The next thing he knew he was near the wall of light. Other exos looked at him but kept marching. They entered the wall of light and disappeared. One bumped into him, nudging him forward.

One of the exos that had been firing at him moved in between his comrades.

"It's coming," Sophie said.

Riley took her by the hand and tried pulling her in between the marching exos, hoping to lose it. Only when the crackling of electric energy began to tingle on his skin did he realize how close to the wall of light he was. Soon he was right up to it and it started to pull on him. He tried turning away but found his feet were locked in place and it was all he could do to stop stumbling backwards into it.

The exo fired, nicking one of its kin. The one it hit turned to look at it. Another shot was fired and Riley jumped back as the blast landed near his feet. Soon he was stumbling back and couldn't stop himself, pulling Sophie along with him.

The tingling on his skin grew all the more fierce and the next thing he knew he was surrounded by blue light, the room with the exos gone from view.

Other exos emerged into this place of blue light and were marching toward him.

Nowhere to turn, Riley pulled Sophie against him and shoved her forward. He was right behind her and they ran into the light.

◆ ◆ ◆

Nick and Grayson followed the officers and they led them through a door which opened up onto a catwalk that led down into a room with this strange wall of blue light.

Lines of black exo-suits marched through.

"Nick?" Grayson said, obviously at a loss.

Metal screeched on metal as the doors on the sides of the room opened up and a half dozen mech-bots on each side began to file in behind the last of the black exos that were walking right into this blue wall. They were all heavily-armed, equipped with cannons and rockets and no doubt an assortment of smaller weapons.

Men in lab coats were around a black—gun—thing pointed at the wall that kept feeding this strange blue energy into it.

The mech-bots marched, one heavy footfall after another, then finished getting in formation behind the final line of black exos entering the wall.

Electricity crackled on the air.

Nick didn't know what to make of it.

The officers they'd been chasing took a lift down to the room and ran on ahead of the mech-bots into the wall of light.

"What's going on?" Grayson said.

"Where are they marching to?" he said.

The last of the mech-bots entered the wall of light. Once they were through, the scientists below started crowding around the gun thing. Not long after, the beam shut off and the blue wall of light began to grow dimmer. Waves of what looked like liquid silver began to appear and coalesce into a giant metallic sphere. The wall of light faded away and the sphere came together completely. It was spinning. Completely transfixed, Nick watched it until it stopped moving and the cracks in it were revealed.

"Nick, what just happened?" Grayson asked.

"I don't know," he said.

She was silent for a moment. "We need to regroup."

"Roger."

Then, as if fully coming around, "Riley and Sophie."

17

INSIDE THE WALL of blue light, the sound of rapid plasma fire quickly rose on the air. Riley hadn't heard this much exchange since the war.

The light ahead of him began to fade and a city street came into view. The sound of giant mech-bots stomping on the ground filled his ears as did the stench of smoke from the burning buildings around them.

Riley and Sophie ran out of the light and stopped in their tracks.

"What—" Riley said.

The black exos started crowding in behind them. A few opened fire. He took Sophie by the hand and the two ran off down the street, dodging to the side as the plasma bursts missed them. They rounded a corner and ran into an alley. From the street, the black enemy exos opened fire, taking down green and gray exos. The mech-bots that had come through the wall of light blasted their way through the throng of oncoming green and gray exo-suited soldiers. They also opened fire on the towering mech-bots on the street, a couple of which Riley recognized as Gambits.

"What's going on!" Sophie shouted above the din of warfare.

"I don't—I don't know."

An enemy exo coming up where the alley met the street spotted them and opened fire. The shot landed by Riley's feet. He returned fire, as did Sophie. Their plasma bursts struck the exo and the thing fell.

"Come on, let's go," he said and grabbed her by the arm, shoving her further down the alley. If anything happened to her—

They ran a couple of blocks.

"We need to find cover," Sophie said.

They turned a corner and ducked into another alley. This one was next to a parkade.

"This way," Riley said and led her into it. The ground shook from the warfare. Plasma fire was heard on the air as was barrage after barrage of bullets. They ran into the base level of the parkade. "Come on." He pulled her toward the stairwell at the far end. Once they got there, they ran up the stairs, passing the exits to the four other levels before they emerged on the roof.

"We're out in the open!" she said.

"We need to assess."

"Can't we do that someplace quieter?"

He ignored the question and surveyed the parkade roof. Three vehicles were up here, one smoking, another a burnt carcass of its former self. Only one vehicle was left intact. He took her to the parkade's edge. From up here, he could see the city streets. He could no longer see the wall of light even though he was looking in its direction.

Giant mech-bots stomped through the streets, their heavy footfalls shaking the ground and sending vibrations even all the way up to where Riley and Sophie stood.

One of the mech-bots, a Gambit, opened fire on one of the mechs that had come through the wall. Its cannon fire ricocheted off the enemy bot as did the heavy torrent of bullets it sent its way. The enemy bot adjusted its mechanical arms and launched a rocket at the Gambit. The rocket struck its hull, lodged itself in the metal, and exploded. The Gambit went up in a fireball and teetered on its legs. A moment later it came crashing down in a fiery heap.

Exo soldiers flew through the air, some doing a sweep of the area, others shooting their cannons at the others fighting on the street below. A couple streaked past the parkade. Riley half-expected for them to turn around because they saw him and Sophie, but they never did and sped on toward the battle on the street.

Explosions boomed through the air. A loud crash alerted Riley's attention to the right and he saw a mech-bot he didn't recognize slam into the side of a building, crumbling the cement and breaking into it so badly he could see the metal framing even from where he stood.

Below, hover tanks drove through the streets, four of them. He recognized them as belonging to the Expherions. Friendlies.

"What's happening?" he whispered slowly.

The tanks below opened fire on another of the mech-bots. This one looked unfamiliar as well, but it stood some fifteen stories tall. There had been so many varieties during the war and seeing this one took Riley back to it. The cannon fire from the tanks shot at the mech-bot's legs, a few shots making their way all the way to the rectangle-like body of the giant machine. A pair of cannons drew up and over the mech-bot's shoulders and opened fire on the tanks. A couple of the tanks went up in the air, whereas the other two drove through the smoke and dust and kept firing. The mech-bot stomped over to one of them and stepped right on it, then turned and blasted the other tank. The other tank stopped its advance. The mech-bot stepped toward it and crushed it beneath its feet.

"What's going on, Riley, what's happening? Where are we?" Sophie asked.

"I don't know. We're in the city. I recognize the buildings." He glanced around. Many of the buildings sported holes in them. Chunks were missing off the edges of some. A couple had collapsed and sat in giant heaps of cement, steel and rubble.

"How can we be in the city? What was that thing? A transporter of some kind?"

"Yeah, I guess. We went through and wound up here."

"There was no fighting in the city when we left. It was quiet. There's an all-out war going on."

An explosion made them both buckle at the knees and they had to put their arms out to brace themselves. "I can see that, Sophie, I'm not stupid!"

She looked at him, eyes wide.

"Sorry. Bad timing. My fault. Listen, let's get down from here. We need to go someplace quieter and figure this out." He checked the readout on his rifle. Plasma levels were down to thirty-percent.

She only nodded. She was obviously mad at his comment. He hadn't meant to snap at her, just with the building rocking at the same time, the confusion, the fighting—it got the better of him.

They headed back the way they had come. Once at the stairwell, he thought about letting her go first—a gentleman thing, maybe a small way to start making it up to her—then thought better of it. If they were to run into trouble, he wanted it to greet him first.

Once at street level, the only thing Riley could think of to do was move as far away from the battle as possible. They'd have to move quickly and stay out of sight as much as possible as well.

He replayed what he saw from the parkade roof in his mind. What were Gambits doing here? Or Expherion soldiers? How could they have left that hangar in the hills and suddenly find themselves in the city with an all-out battle going on? He thought maybe something had erupted while he and Sophie had been captured. Perhaps Commander Tiel had sent in a team to find them and they had been intercepted and one thing led to another until an assault from both sides blew out.

What he did know for right now was that he and Sophie weren't safe, especially since their only protection were a couple of plasma rifles in the middle of a warzone. They ran down the alley, getting further and further away from the battle. A few more exo-soldiers flew by overhead. More explosions rocked the air. Bullet fire was everywhere, the rat-a-tat-tat of machine and Gatling guns drumming their steady rhythms into his racing heart. He glanced at Sophie. She had worry written all over her face. He felt bad again for snapping at her.

They came up on another street. The battle was here, too, this one between exo-soldiers. One in black was bounding down the street then jumped into the air and landed on top of a green one. It rained blow after blow upon it before jumping back and rapidly firing its weapon. When the barrage was over, the green one lay in a mangled heap on the ground.

A group of gray exo-soldiers were firing on a group of four black ones, picking them off. The shots from the gray ones came like a wall of plasma fire, slamming into the black ones and knocking them down. Other exos fought in the street hand-to-hand, swinging their cannon arms around like baseball bats, banging into each other.

"Let's go back the way we came," he told Sophie, and the two double backed a bit before turning down another alley and emerging onto another street. Here, vehicles were on fire, as were a few of the buildings, smoke billowing out of the windows.

Riley peered up and down the street, then took Sophie's hand again and pulled her across it. She didn't resist him and he took that as a good sign. Either that or she was so panicked she didn't care. But Sophie was a trained soldier, prepared for warfare. Seeing all this, even being thrust in the middle of it, should be okay for her.

Can never be fully prepared for war, he supposed.

They entered another alley and the sound of weapon fire was further behind them.

A black exo flew in and landed behind them, slamming Riley between the shoulder blades. He went flying forward and skidded along the ground, scraping his forearms and knees. Sophie was knocked to the side.

"Don't move," the exo said.

Riley was stuck on all fours, his weapon . . . where was it? It had been knocked from his hands in the fall.

Plasma fire went off and he looked over his shoulder. Sophie had taken the thing down. She marched up to it and opened fire on the exo's head unit, sending shot after shot straight into it.

Screaming, she gave it all she had.

"Sophie!" Riley shouted and got off his hands and knees. The skin along his forearms stung as did his knee caps. He hobbled over to Sophie and wrapped his arms around her from behind, pulling her away. She kept firing. "Sophie, stop!" He knocked the rifle from her hands and it hit the ground.

She faced him and screamed. Then her face scrunched and the tears began to fall.

He pulled her in and held her. "It's okay. It's okay. It's over."

She wept in his arms. He held her tight.

Panic, he thought. It was no doubt a culmination of the past week, trying to escape the hills with their lives, then suddenly finding themselves here. He couldn't blame her. He needed a reprieve, too.

She finally stopped after a few minutes and pulled away. Without saying anything, she bent down and picked up her weapon. She looked at him once then looked away and started down the alley.

Guess she doesn't want to talk about it, he thought. *This isn't the place anyway.* He looked around for his rifle and saw it lying off to the side.

Wincing as he rubbed his elbows, he went over and picked it up.

Then went after her.

18

THE CITY

THEY WERE FAR away from the battle now, coming up on an area that used to be known as The Forks, where the Assiniboine River met the Red. It had been a major hub throughout its history, first for trading then, as modern times came, for shopping and taking one's kids, too. It lasted that way until World War III. Then it became an outpost for the Canadian Forces. Later, it was abandoned.

Walking amongst the empty buildings, Riley was relieved to see that, so far, they were still standing. Which shouldn't be. These buildings were demolished during the war.

"Something's not right," he said. "These buildings shouldn't be here."

"I know," she said. "Where are we?" At least she was talking. He wanted to see how she was doing, ask her how she was feeling, but didn't think this was the time.

So he said, "This is Winnipeg. The buildings are the same. I've been pulling us around because I know the streets."

"That transporter . . . did it take us to an alternate, I don't know, dimension or something?"

"It'd be amazing if it did." They kept walking, getting closer to the river. They took the steps leading down to the walking path. "I mean, amazing in that something like that . . . I don't even have the words."

The sounds of explosions were still on the air, but further away now.

Up ahead was a bridge that used to run over the river. Now it was blasted in half. It looked like the fighting had made its way over here, too.

Fighter jets roared overhead. Riley followed their flight path and saw they were headed toward the action in the city. They made a pass, circled around, then streamed in and something dropped from one of them. A moment later a huge explosion sounded on the air, making him cover his ears. Sophie had done the same.

"Friend or foe?" she asked.

"Who can tell?" he said, but didn't know if she heard him amidst the explosion's echo. He waited for the sound to taper off before he said, "We can't stay here. We need to keep moving. Need to find some solid ground." He held the rifle aloft then leaned it on his shoulder. Sophie held her weapon like a cane.

"Agreed." She paused, then said, "I'm scared, Riley. I don't know what's happening."

"Then it's time we get some answers. We head back to base."

They started walking.

"I'm sure Commander Tiel will be thrilled to see us," she said.

"Probably thinks we're dead. I doubt he's going to believe what happened to us, with that wall of light and everything."

The two moved on, following the river. They'd have to go back near the battle zone to get to Stake 48. Riley decided they could use the cover of the trees lining the river's path to their advantage. As dirty as it was, the water looked inviting. He was so thirsty and assumed Sophie was, too. He also didn't want to get sick so abstained from gathering a sip.

Gun and plasma fire was heard over the trees as were the whistles of launching rockets. Each time an explosion went off, it echoed in Riley's chest.

The two kept walking. After about ten minutes, the path ended and curved back in toward The Forks. It would have to be along the riverbank from here. Some of the trees were knocked over from whatever mech-bots that had once traversed here. Across the river beside them, a couple of the buildings were on fire. It appeared the battle had been moving from one part of the city to the next as each side retreated or advanced.

Riley thought back to that wall of light, its brilliant luminance, the sharp electric tingles on his skin. What was that thing? A super weapon of the enemy? A transporter? He recalled what Tiel had said about the particle accelerator and one of its intended uses: the ability to move in and out of enemy territory as conveniently as walking through a door. Had the enemy succeeded in completing that design? To be able to move in and out of warzones like that would certainly protect one's troops while en route to the desired area. No ambushes or sneak attacks. The fact that, as evidenced by his and Sophie's going through it, unarmoured humans could use it was mind blowing. Did Tiel know about this? Was that why he had been so secretive about it at the start? How did the enemy know to make a transporter out of it?

Riley needed answers, especially given the war sounding past the trees.

Something caught his eye. He grabbed Sophie and pulled her down against the base of one of the trees.

"Don't move," he whispered. He peered around the tree trunk. Three black exos were making their way through the woods.

Him and Sophie remained perfectly still and waited for the exos to pass. He even waited an extra minute to make sure they were gone before standing up and moving again. They walked on, stepping around fallen bushes and trees. The scent of smoke filled his nostrils and soon the smoke itself bathed the area in gray. Coughing, he looked for the source of the flame but couldn't see any.

"Be careful," he said.

"Should we turn back?"

"Keep going." He pulled the collar of his shirt up over his mouth. Sophie did the same.

The smoke grew thicker and thicker with each step. To the left he heard the roar of a fire and started to feel its heat. He steered them close to the riverbank, nearly right at the edge, to maintain some distance.

Plasma fire streamed out of the smoke, zipping past them.

"Run!" he said, and the two sprinted as fast as they could down the riverbank, sidestepping the rocks and washed up broken branches and driftwood.

Riley fired off his rifle into the smoke, hoping he hit whoever had just opened fire on them.

They kept running. Heavy footfalls nearby told him someone was keeping pace with them. Maybe more than one.

He checked his readout on the rifle. Plasma levels were at twenty-seven percent. He'd have to be careful lest he waste any.

Up ahead, a black exo emerged from the smoke and aimed its cannon at them. Both Riley and Sophie fired at it, the simultaneous shots hitting it in the chest and legs, knocking it down. Riley pounced on it and shoved the barrel of his rifle right into its face and let loose two more shots. Sparks flew, some landed on his hands, stinging them.

"Any more?" Sophie asked.

"Don't know. Keep an eye out."

He got off the exo and kept moving.

The smoke dried out his mouth and a sharp pinch formed at the back of his throat. Coughing, he wished for something to drink.

They kept moving and saw the shadows of other exos traversing throughout the smoke. Doubling back wasn't an option. He guessed these exos were on perimeter control, moving up and down the riverbank a part of that.

He checked Sophie. She looked worn and haggard. She walked with one hand covering her mouth, the other holding her weapon.

They came to a part where a giant tree had fallen over and ran off the bank into the river. It was hard to see where the tree started in the smoke so one by one they climbed over it. He went up on it first for a lookout and, when from what he could tell the coast was clear, pulled her up beside him. He hopped down on the other side, landing with a thud. Sophie dropped beside him.

Hopefully the smoke would begin to clear soon.

Another stream of plasma fire started their way as did gunfire.

Like before, he told her to run. A moving target was much more difficult to hit. He wished he could see his attackers. Surely then he'd be able to fire off the necessary shots to take them down.

The plasma fire grew thicker and one struck Sophie in the shoulder, knocking her to the ground.

"No!" he shouted. He got down beside her.

She was unconscious.

Quickly, he picked her up, put her over his shoulder, holding one rifle with the same hand keeping her balanced, the other rifle in his left hand. He wouldn't be able to use them like this, but at least he had her and the weapons.

Riley moved as quickly as he could.

The plasma fire grew so thick that one nicked his leg, causing it to go numb.

Grunting, he had only one choice. Limping, he waded into the river. Within a few feet of the shore, he went under, Sophie with him. He dropped one of the rifles and tried surfacing with just the one hand. It wasn't enough. He had to let go of the other one, too. Heart sinking as their only defense sunk to the river's floor, he got his hands under Sophie's armpits and kicked upward. When he broke the surface, they went under again. He did the same thing and they emerged above the water.

He got one arm beneath Sophie and leaned her on him, and used the other to paddle a little further out. Hopefully between most of their bodies submerged in water and the smoke cover, they were safe.

He checked for Sophie's breathing. It was there, just a little. He hoped she hadn't inhaled too much water when they went under, that somehow her subconscious was still functioning and she had held her breath.

Slowly, he swam with her, waiting for the smoke to thin.

19

THE RIVERBANK

About ten minutes later, the smoke began to fade and eventually Riley pulled Sophie back to shore. The second he climbed on dry land, he laid her out and put his ear to her mouth. She had stopped breathing.

"Nonononono," he said and immediately got to work pressing on her chest. He pressed down three times in quick succession, then pinched her nose and blew into her mouth. He put his ear by her lips.

Nothing.

"Come on," he said. One, two, three, blow.

He listened again.

Still nothing.

"Come on, Sophie, wake up!" One, two, three, blow.

Nothing again.

Grunting, he pressed down on her chest even harder than he meant to. He blew into her mouth fairly hard, too.

He tilted her head to the side when she coughed up some water. When she was done, he gently lifted her head. Her eyes slowly opened and she groaned.

"You're okay, you're okay," he reassured her. "Thank God you're okay."

"Wha—what happened?"

He caught his breath, then said, "We went for a little swim."

"I'm cold," she said, shaking.

He scooped her up and held her in his arms, rocking her back and forth. She didn't return the embrace but instead had her arms folded in between her body and his. "It's okay, Sophie. It's over. I'm so happy you're alive."

"Me . . . me, too," she said.

They stayed by the foot of the river for a little while as he waited for her to fully come around. Inspecting her shoulder, he saw the plasma burn. He hoped the river's water helped calm it a little.

"Think you could walk?" he asked her.

She nodded and he helped her get up. She held her arms, shivering. "Where's my gun?"

"We had to lose them to get away. Didn't have a choice."

"Oh." She looked as if she was going to say more but couldn't find the words.

He put his arm around her shoulder. "Come on," he said, "let's get moving."

They walked along the riverbank in silence except for when Riley periodically checked in on her. Aside from the burn and being shook up, she was okay. As for himself, he was sore all over, still recovering from the beating he took earlier and all the action since. His leg hurt, too. There would be time for rest later, though. Right now they needed to get back to base.

By the time they were past the city and well into the suburbs, it was getting late. The sun was on the verge of going down. He hoped they would make it there before dark.

He turned into the forest lining the riverbank and the two made their way up the hill to more level ground. Soon they came out onto a suburban street. He thought he would see signs of life. While the city had been evacuated during the war, people had returned afterward and began to repopulate. But right now, it seemed everyone was indoors. Not every house was standing either. Some sat in piles of wood and cement. A few others still stood, but were covered in burn marks and had open windows.

He directed Sophie to the nearest sidewalk and they began walking. Sounds of the battle downtown were barely heard now.

Stake 48 should be coming up soon. It was maybe fifteen more minutes' walk from here. They kept on. Riley kept an eye out for any exos. A tank was coming toward them down the street. It looked like a friendly but he couldn't be one hundred percent sure from this far away. Him and Sophie went into someone's backyard and hid behind the fence, waiting for it to pass.

"How are you holding up?" he asked her.

"I'll live. Shoulder doesn't hurt as much now. Think it's already starting to scab over. It still stings, though."

"It's probably going to for a while."

Once the tank rolled past, they got back on the sidewalk and continued. A couple more times they had to hide in pedestrian yards as tanks and hover jeeps made their way past on the street. One of them that went past belonged to their own. Riley thought about flagging them down but by the time he had stood and rounded the fence to make good on it, it was already too far down the street to see them. He wasn't going to go running and yelling after it and draw attention to his position for any possible enemy soldiers or exos.

"Stake 48 should be just down here," he said and they headed down the street. He kept an eye out for it . . . but didn't see it.

"Isn't it—" Sophie started.

"What?" The area was empty. There was no base. "I'm sure we're in the right spot. Been coming and going from here for over a year."

"There's no building," she said.

"Yeah, I can see that!" he snapped. Then, "Sorry. Just tired and frustrated."

"It's okay. I'm angry, too." She started pacing.

"I don't understand," he said. "We're in the right place, yeah?"

"Absolutely. I know my way around here like nobody's business. We *are* in the right place, Riley."

"Then where is it?"

Sophie stopped pacing then turned to him. Her eyes were wide. "It hasn't been built yet."

20

"WHAT DO YOU mean it hasn't been built yet?" Riley asked. His head hurt, the events of the day catching up with him.

"Come on, Riley, put it together!" She pressed her lips tightly together. "Sorry. I'm just tired."

"It's okay."

She came up to him. "It makes sense now: the particle accelerator, the wall of light, walking into the middle of a warzone and, now, Stake 48 not being here. It wasn't a transporter. It was . . . it was a time machine."

Was she serious? But, she did have a point. Several, actually. "I don't know what to say, but it makes sense. So, what, we're in the past?"

"Seems that way. Manta Six figured out how to bend Space and Time to their will and then transported troops back in time to give them an edge in the war."

"If that's true, then at what point are we?"

"I don't know. We could be right at the beginning or right in the middle of it. Could be at the tail end, for all we know."

It was hard to get his head around it. Time travel . . . did such a thing even exist?

Evidently.

"Well, let's play the game, then," he said. "Let's say they succeed and tip the war in their favor . . . wouldn't that mean these events have already happened and, if so, where we came from would have already been changed?

Is our . . . future . . . where we were . . . the outcome of all this?"

"That they lost anyway?"

He nodded. "Yeah."

"I don't know. I'm not a quantum physicist. Maybe Time is linear regardless of tampering with the time stream. For example, what happens still happens in order: we won, they go back, they change things, *then* the future changes. We live our lives up to—" Her eyes went wide. "How do we get back?"

"We'd need their machine."

"It's not like we can just waltz up to the enemy and ask for a ride home. Are we stuck here?"

"Okay, slow down. I honestly don't know. I'm still coming to grips with the idea that we're in the past never mind getting back. Let's just take this one thing at a time."

She began massaging her temples with her thumb and index finger.

"How are you feeling?" he asked.

"Aside from confused? Just tired and sore. How 'bout you?"

"Same." He took a deep breath. The fatigue had caught up with him and a tired headache was forming behind his eyes. What he'd give for a place to lay his head and a bite to eat.

"The past," she said. "I can't believe it."

"Me neither. This isn't anything we've been trained for. This is totally new ground."

She finally took her hand away from her temples, then ran her fingers through her hair, pushing it back from her forehead. "What's our play?"

He thought about it for a moment. "I think we need to look at the facts and try to stay as calm as possible.

Let's try to keep it simple so we don't start freaking out over the ramifications of being here."

"Agreed. Simple is good."

"Okay, fact one: we're in the past. Let's just say that's normal for the sake of this discussion." *Normal. Yeah, right.* "Fact two: we don't know *when* we are. We need to find out. We can try and find a data stream of some kind, get today's date."

"Okay. And if we can't find one?"

"I said let's just keep it simple. The next task would be to find out when we are. After that, is fact three: we need to get home. How? Who knows? Again, let's keep it simple."

"What about changes to the timeline?"

"I know, but, again—"

"Yeah, yeah, keep it simple."

"We have to, Sophie. The first rule in a panic situation is to try and stay calm. How do we do that? By not getting overwhelmed with the details. Let's take things as they come."

"So is it wrong to try and plan for step three at this stage?"

"It's not wrong, but I don't think it's wise. What I do know is—" More tanks turned down the street. "Let's go," he said and the two crossed the lot of where Stake 48 would one day stand. They headed down a side street and heard shouting from behind them.

"They saw us!" she said.

"Keep running."

They ran past several houses. Riley looked over his shoulder. One of the tanks had turned down the street. A couple soldiers were running after them on foot.

"Step on it!" he told her and he dug in, giving it all he had. His leg was pretty much fine now. It seemed she was still weak from the plasma shot as she had a hard time keeping up. He was forced to slow down to accommodate her. They turned up someone's driveway and came up to a metal-grated fence. He searched for the lock so the door would open, but it was operated by code. They had no choice but to climb it.

"Here," he said and wove his fingers together, cupping his hands so he could give her a boost.

She stuck her foot in his hands and he hoisted her up. She climbed over the fence. He followed by grabbing the top of the fence and pressing himself up so he could get his leg over, straddling it. Once pulling his other leg around, he hopped down. They ran to the far side of the yard and hid behind a shed. Soon, footfalls drew nearer.

"They're here," he whispered. Without any weapons, there was no way they'd last in a hand-to-hand fight.

Behind them was more fencing. They'd have to hop it.

He gave her a nudge and nodded toward the fence. She nodded back. They stood and he heard the soldiers climb the fence and enter the yard.

A moment later, "Don't move!" The soldier had a handheld aimed at them.

Riley put his hands up. Sophie did the same.

A second soldier came up beside the first, weapon drawn as well. Judging by the soldiers' uniforms, they were one of their own: Expherions.

"Put your hands on your head and get on your knees," the first soldier barked. When he took a step closer, Riley read his nametag: Rogers.

Riley obeyed, as did Sophie.

"You're making a mistake," Riley said. "We are not your enemy. We're one of you."

Sophie shot him a look that said he shouldn't have said anything.

"Look at my pants," Riley said. "They're the same as yours. We're on the same team."

"What are you doing?" Sophie whispered. Her words were sharp.

He knew she was referring to interacting with people from the past and the effect it could have on the future. It was a little late for that. With Manta Six from the future showing up and engaging in battle, the timeline had already been polluted. That was assuming the future they came from wasn't a result of Manta Six's tampering already. If it was . . . he didn't want to think about it. Right now he was more concerned about getting arrested for no reason.

"Citizens are to be evacuated. Is this your residence, sir?" Rogers asked.

"No. I just said we're on the same team. Look at what I'm wearing, at what she's wearing!"

"Then show me some identification. Wearing officer fatigues doesn't make you one of us. You could've swiped them from a dead body, for all we know. You're covered in filth and you smell terrible. On your feet."

Riley slumped his shoulders, feigning resignation. It seemed to have worked because the second soldier lowered his weapon slightly. Quickly, Riley spun around, disarmed Rogers and took the weapon in his own hands. He spun back and fired, shooting the other soldier down with a burst of electricity. He turned and Rogers tried to grab him but Sophie came in and rammed him with her shoulder, knocking him down. He took her to the ground with him and punched her in the kidney.

"Stop!" Riley shouted, his weapon aimed straight at Rogers. "Let her go."

The man showed his palms and Sophie rolled off him. She staggered a bit when she got to her feet.

"I don't want any trouble," Riley said. "We're not your enemy."

Sophie went and inspected the other soldier. "He's alive."

Good thing, Riley thought. The weapons must've been set to stun versus kill. And they should have been if an arrest was all these guys were trying to do anyway. Sophie bent down and picked up the other soldier's weapon. *Keep it simple.* "I'm sorry," he told the officer then shot him in the chest. The man's body jerked when the electricity struck him.

"You realize we'll be wanted," she said.

"I know."

"The soldiers on the street . . . they'll come looking for them."

"That's why we can't be here when they come." He put the handheld behind him in the band of his pants. "Come on. Let's get out of here."

21

THE SUBURBS

WITH ONE HAND on the handheld, Sophie pinched the bridge of her nose with the other. That was the last time she ever wanted to take a plasma shot. It totally messed with your system, knocking you out, burning you, making you groggy afterward. She did her best to bite back the headache pressing against her temples.

They had walked for about half an hour, staying out of sight of any military vehicles that passed through.

Riley shouldn't have shot those officers. Now there was no doubt an alert out on them.

They needed answers, but there was no one to turn to. She was still having a hard time coming to grips with the reality they had just traveled through Time and were now at some point in the past during the war. She wished she knew when, not that that would make things any easier. The main thing was getting back home—back where they belonged—but she did her best to stick to Riley's principle of keeping it simple. The next step was trying to find out *when* they were. The hard part was that with the city evacuated there would be no point to having any news service. There wouldn't be any one to report the news anyway. The only source would be their own officers, but to talk to them without getting arrested—

"Do you remember when the evacuation took place?" Sophie asked.

"It was right after things showed signs of escalating and the mech-bots started getting used. I don't remember the exact date, but the year was 2079. It could be 2079 right now, or sometime later. Maybe if I thought about it, the date or even month would come to mind. Just feeling out of sorts at the moment."

"I hear ya. Me, too." She looked at the weapon she held in her hand. It matched Riley's, a standard issue stun pistol capable of firing electricity into an opponent. It was meant to force an attacker to the ground but not do any permanent damage unless desired. People at the base called it "the stunner" but its real name was the Taze 150. It worked similar to a regular handheld by firing the electrical charge in a clean burst. The burst would then strike the opponent and spread out over their body, taking them to the ground. She kept a firm grip on it. "How are you holding up?"

"Fine. Sore, like before," he said, "but I'm getting a second wind. I'll manage. You?"

"Just a headache and my shoulder still hurts. I'll live, though."

"Going to have to." He nodded up the street. "We'll turn there and make our way up the next one."

"Any idea where we're going?"

"I'm leading us further into the burbs. I figure with all the action focused downtown, the further out we can be from it, the better."

They kept on and turned right at the upcoming street. After a few seconds of being down it, a jet roared overhead, heading downtown. Sophie instinctively stopped in her tracks.

"What's wrong?" he asked.

"Nothing, just reflex. Sorry."

"Don't be sorry," he said as they continued on. "I'm jittery, too. Would give anything for a soft couch and some serious nap time."

"Agreed."

"That's actually not a bad idea," he said. "Any one of these houses will do. We should go in and hunker down in a basement and grab some shut eye, clear our heads."

"Sounds good to me. Which one?"

He looked up and down the street. She didn't care which one he picked as long as whatever one had a comfortable bed and some food. "We'll take the brown one, the second one in from the corner."

"Fine by me."

They headed there. As they approached the house, plasma fire streamed in their direction.

"Are you kidding me?" Riley shouted.

Never a break, she thought. She looked in the direction of the plasma fire and saw two green exos hovering just above the street, coming toward them. She considered using the stunner, but doubted it would do any good against the exos' armor.

They ran, rounding a parked vehicle and getting in between the houses, making it more difficult for the exos to see where they had gone. They hopped a fence just as a couple of plasma bursts missed them. She accidentally dropped her stunner. She rolled along the ground, doubled back a few feet, grabbed it, then was back up, running after Riley who was about ten feet ahead.

"Keep hopping fences," he said. "Stay low when you land."

"Got it."

They came up to the next fence. This one she could manage on her own and hoisted herself up and over. They were in another backyard, this one belonging to a bi-level. A dual glass patio door led out onto the deck attached to the house.

The exos came in fast behind them and flew over the fence. They sent plasma bursts forward. Sophie rolled off to the side, as did Riley. The bursts missed them and crashed through the patio doors. Having no choice but to go forward, they ran into the house and found themselves in the living room. Sophie veered off to the right, into the kitchen. Just past it to the right was a hallway leading to bedrooms. In front of her a door ran off the kitchen and led into the dining room. She heard footfalls rushing on stairs and assumed they belonged to Riley.

The exos flew into the living room. Sophie ducked as a plasma burst came her way. She returned fire with the stunner. The electrical burst struck the exo and crackled over its armor, not fazing it.

Had they been in their own timeline, these guys would've been friendlies, but here—she was sure her and Riley were counted as wanted men given what happened with those other soldiers.

She turned into the dining room and saw the front landing just beyond. If she could just reach the door—

The exo came up behind her, cannon raised.

◆ ◆ ◆

Riley made it to the top of the stairs. There were a couple rooms up here and a bathroom.

"Stupid, stupid, stupid," he muttered. There was no way out except either through a window or going back down the stairs straight into the lion's mouth. *Sophie* . . .

He moved to the nearest room as he heard the whirring of the exo's thrusters taking the soldier up the stairs. Should he surrender? These guys were not the enemy after all. He just didn't want to get shot down on sight.

He emerged in what looked like a den. There was only one small window leading out.

"Okay, okay, think!" The exo would be here any second. "Yes!" He saw a gun cabinet behind the desk in the center of the room. It was locked with a code box. There would be no way he'd guess the combination.

He aimed the stunner at the code box.

♦ ♦ ♦

Sophie was on her knees in the foyer, hands over her head.

"Let's see some identification," the exo told her.

"I don't have any."

"What's your name?"

She didn't know if she should give it or make something up. *Umm* . . . "Ella."

"Ella, you are wanted on account of opening fire at two armed officers and for being present in an evacuated zone. You are requested to come with us."

Sophie kept her ears open, listening for any movement at the top of the house.

She hoped Riley was all right.

♦ ♦ ♦

The exo killed its thrusters and landed on the floor with a thud. It entered the room, its head unit breaking through the top of the doorframe. It scanned the area. When it didn't find anyone, it rotated its torso side-to-side, seeming to double check things.

Riley was on the roof just outside the window. The stunner had scrambled the code box's circuits, rendering it useless. The exo moved further into the room and went to the closet in the corner. With a giant strike of its arm, it crashed its cannon down on the door, tearing it off its hinges. The closet was empty. Now, with its back turned, Riley took his chance and aimed the plasma rifle at the kill switch at the back of the head unit.

He fired.

The shot hit the exo dead on and the thing dropped.

Riley climbed back in the window and went over to it. The exo unit lay on the ground. He aimed the rifle at it.

"Open it!" he shouted. "I'm not kidding."

The whirring of gears sounded and the front hatch of the exo unit opened, revealing the soldier within.

"Get. Out," Riley said.

The man—a young guy with short-cropped blond hair—climbed out of the suit and stood with his hands raised.

"What's the date?" Riley asked.

"What?" the guy replied.

"Give me today's date."

"June seventh."

"The year, too."

"2080." The guy looked at him like he was crazy, which was kind of how he felt at the moment.

"Operating code for your exo unit."

"Not telling."

Not wanting to give the guy an inch, Riley said, "You tell or I shoot."

"I won't let it fall into enemy hands."

Riley struck him in the forehead with the butt of the rifle. The guy dropped to his knees. "Operating code. Now!"

"Never."

Riley clubbed him again, this time right on the vertebrae. "Next I burn you."

"Then burn me."

If he shot him, the guy would go unconscious and he'd never get the code. He needed the suit, so he clubbed the soldier again then got down beside him and grabbed his arm, putting it in a chicken wing. The guy squealed.

"Give me the operating code!"

The soldier winced.

Riley pulled up on his arm, hyperextending it.

"Ahhh, okay, okay."

"Right now or I break it!"

"Four-seven-nine-eight-eight."

"Enter it."

Not releasing him, Riley only gave the guy the room he needed to crawl over to the suit and enter the code on the keypad within. When it checked out, Riley said, "Thank you," and let the man go. He stood above him then shot him with the rifle. The man fell over onto his side. He'd be out for a while.

Riley went and lay in the suit. He pressed a few buttons and a small covering folded over his legs and hips. Then the top hatch folded over on top of him, covering his chest. He tapped another button and covered his head. Once sealed within, he brought the suit to its feet.

Sophie hated having a cannon aimed at her. She could only hope Riley was okay and he wouldn't find himself with the same fate.

An exo came down the stairs.

The other exo aiming its cannon at Sophie said, "Where is he? I heard a commotion."

"Got away," the other exo said. "Took the window. I tried to pursue" —he kept moving toward the exo— "but he was already part way down the street. He tried firing a weapon at me from that far range but—" The exo unit fired and struck the kill switch of the one that held Sophie at cannon point.

"What the—" she said.

"Get up," the other exo told her. It then turned its cannon on the one that just fell. "Open the suit."

It complied right away and the soldier within was a girl. One couldn't tell through the speakers on the suits.

"Give her your operating code," the exo said, and Sophie put two and two together.

Well done, Riley.

"I will not," the girl said as she climbed out.

"Look," Sophie said, "we don't want any trouble."

"Too late for that," the girl replied. Then, as if finally realizing what was happening, "Mitch?"

"Upstairs, sleeping," Riley said from inside the other exo. "Give us the code and we'll be on our way."

"I can't. I'm not supposed to." She was clearly a rookie. The panic in her eyes gave her away. Perhaps, Sophie thought, she could talk her into giving the code.

"I need your help," Sophie said. "We're just trying to survive this war. We're not out to hurt anyone, but have had to defend ourselves. All we want is to go home. Nothing else."

"I'm sorry, but I can't give you the code."

"Please don't say that. I'll have to make you give it to me, then. I really don't want to do that if I don't have to."

The other woman raised her hands in a fighting stance. Sophie looked to Riley. He took the suit a step back.

Sophie raised her hands, too, and got ready. The woman came in with a swift right hook. Sophie ducked, stepped to the side, and delivered a kick to the woman's stomach, dropping her. She got down on her knees beside her and put the woman's head in her hands. With one hand hooking the jaw, the forearm of the same under her chin, she started to torque the woman's head, putting immense pressure on her neck.

"The code!" Sophie demanded.

"I-I can't . . ."

Sophie put more pressure.

"Okay, okay. Six-three-nine-four-three. Six-three-nine-four-three!"

Sophie put her in a sleeper and laid her out. If only the woman would've listened.

"You should have verified it," Riley said.

"Sorry, I'm not an expert at making people talk."

"Well, who knows, by the time this is all over, you just might be."

22

Sporting their newfound exo armor, Riley and Sophie made their way back onto the streets. They took things slow, careful to stay out of sight when possible. At least now, armed, they could more easily stand their ground against any future attacks.

"Why don't we just fly to wherever it is we're going?" Sophie asked.

"Because A, I don't know where we're going just yet and, B, we run the risk of being shot down by the enemy if we do. I don't really feel like falling to my death today, especially after all that's happened," Riley said.

After a half hour, it was sunset. Soon, Riley would have to switch on the armor's night vision. Hungry and thirsty, he decided to steer them in the direction of a supermarket down the street. There was a chance there might still be some non-perishables on the shelves they could take advantage of. They had tried the pantry of the house but had found nothing.

Soon, Sophie said, "I'm tired of walking."

"You're not walking. The armor is walking for you."

"You know what I mean. We need to come up with a plan."

She was right. They couldn't continue to aimlessly walk around, not after they established *when* they were. The next step in their three-step plan would be to figure out a way back home. But how? Manta Six were the ones who created the vortex. They'd have to go back into enemy camp, somehow locate the device—if it even came through with them, that was—figure out how to work it, then use it to get back. It was a longshot. Worse, it was impossible, it seemed.

"Did you hear me?" she said. "I said we need to—"

"I heard you. The truth is" —he stopped and turned toward her— "I don't have a plan. At least, not yet. The thought of going home—I love it. I want it. I just don't see how it's possible right now."

"We can't do this on our own."

"I know. I don't know if it was the adrenaline or the confusion of the moment that made me think we could, but now that things have slowed down, I'm able to think more clearly and I can't seem to get my head around what we need to do."

"I know. I've been thinking about it, too."

"Have any ideas?"

"Nothing that's not complicated or impossible."

"Perhaps we should—"

The sound of rocket fire caught Riley's attention to up ahead. About a quarter kilometer away, a silver land rover burst forth from the band of trees lining the road and cut across it. He hit the zoom on his visor and activated the night vision. The rover was armed, with two giant arms protruding from on top of either side of the wheel wells. Each acted like a cannon and sent forth rockets into the opposite line of trees. It got off another shot and the rocket exploded inside the band of trees. Flying out from them were a series of black exos like a bunch of disturbed crows. Another rover joined the first and began firing as well.

"We should go back the other way," Riley said. He turned to Sophie and followed her gaze. Not far from where they stood, an armada of green exo soldiers were coming out of the woodwork and marching toward the rovers. "Yeah, we should definitely get out of here."

A jet flew overhead. Riley followed it with the zoom and recognized it as a friendly.

The battle's all the way out here, too, he thought.

Just then another rover screeched out of the darkness, coming in behind them. This one was black and dark gray, much more archaic than its silver counterpart. Riley didn't recognize it as one of their own. When the rover sent a barrage of bullets into the marching green armada, it only confirmed his theory.

"Sophie, look out!" Their comms were tuned in only to each other's frequencies lest they start communicating with the other soldiers. At this point, he wanted to keep their presence a secret.

Sophie dove to the side and crouched. Bullets whizzed by overhead.

Riley ran over to her. "Come on, let's go!"

"Where?"

"Up."

They activated their thrusters and took off into the air. As they ascended, streams of plasma fire followed them from the ground as did bursts of plasma from across them as black exos fired.

Riley returned fire, aiming his cannon at every shadow he saw. He started to take some of them out, knocking them from the sky and sending them tumbling to the earth below. Sophie was doing the same.

"We need to separate!" Riley said.

"Copy."

They veered off one from the other. As Riley flew through the air, he fired at every black exo that came across his scanner. A blast hit him in the legs from behind and sent him tumbling. He grabbed the controls inside the arm unit and manipulated them to slow his descent. He came to a full stop and hovered. He looked through his visor for Sophie, but couldn't see her. He checked his scanner. Her signal was lost amidst all the other exos it was tracking, including friendlies.

Shouldn't have separated, he thought. But they really didn't have a choice. Together, they were a bigger target, but now that they were on their own, he couldn't just up and leave the battlefield. He had no choice but to fight.

He flew down and avoided getting hit by a rocket coming from the enemy rover. He fired at it with his cannon. The shot hit it dead on but was absorbed by the shielding of its hull. He knew from past experience the armor on the rovers was tough and it took a series of concentrated blasts to breach it.

All around, exo soldiers exchanged fire both in the air and on the ground. The silver rovers let off a stream of bullets, attacking any approaching black exos.

Riley flew to ground level and killed his thrusters. A black exo was coming toward him. He fired plasma at it then followed up with a single shot of the half-dozen. The explosion rocked the enemy suit and brought it down. He turned and did the same to another closing in. He ignited the thrusters, rose up a little, then aimed his cannon at a semi-circle of enemy exos closing in on two friendlies. He adjusted the plasma and instead of firing off single bursts, it came out as a solid stream and he sent it into the semi-circle like a flamethrower. He did one swipe of the group then came back and did it again. He followed up a third time and took them down.

Soon more green exos joined them.

The rovers up ahead moved and spun around a hundred and eighty degrees, setting themselves up to take out a batch of new enemies coming in from the other side.

Bullets rained around Riley as they pinged and ricocheted off his suit. He looked for the source and saw a lone exo firing at him. He let off another one of the half-dozen. He missed and it landed at the exo's feet. The explosion was enough to stagger it so he swooped in and tackled it to the ground. He hammered on it with his cannon like a caveman trying to crack open a coconut with a stick. Sparks flew, then he aimed his cannon at the head unit and fired.

The enemy rover sent off a rocket toward one of the silver ones. The explosion wreaked serious damage to the friendly rover.

Riley flew over to the enemy one and started firing blast after blast into it. Metal flaps opened on the rover and it sent out a series of plasma bursts. Riley turned tail and got some distance. A couple other green exos joined him and together they fired at the enemy rover, each focusing their plasma cannons in one continuous stream. They concentrated the plasma into a single area and soon the hull began to give way and melt. They stopped as more bursts came in their direction and got out of the way, then quickly resumed their attack, this time focusing their streams on the cockpit. Soon, it began to melt, the hot molten metal no doubt collapsing in on the pilot.

The rover stopped firing.

The greens blasted it a bit longer then stopped.

Another black rover showed up.

Sophie killed her thrusters and let herself drop down onto the black exo beneath her feet, crushing its chest unit. She fired her cannon into the head several times. Sparks flew and black scorch marks appeared on the enemy exo's hull.

The remaining silver rover sent plasma bursts into the battle, taking out the enemy. Green exos battled it out on the ground, some in the air.

"Riley, do you copy? Where are you?" she said into the comm.

"Over by the enemy rover. We could use some help."

"I'm coming. Give me a sec, though."

"Roger."

She was about to take off when a black exo crashed into her from the side and pinned her to the ground. She kicked on her thrusters and moved along the ground, getting out from under it. She turned them off, stood, then dove forward, igniting them again. She plowed into the enemy exo like a battering ram and crashed it into the ground. She sent repeated plasma shots into it and smashed it with her cannon. She was glad for the cannon's armored outer casing so she could wield it like a baseball bat; it could take the abuse.

A green exo came up beside her and blasted away one of the two enemy exos approaching her. She fired on the other one and the green exo joined her; together they took it down.

She wanted to say thanks but wasn't tuned into its frequency. She made the adjustment and got on the regular comm. channel.

"Thanks," she said.

The other exo didn't motion that it acknowledged her, but no matter.

She took off into the air and surveyed the scene below. Green and black exos duked it out on the ground. A few more battled it out in the air. The black enemy rover was pulled up beside the smoking heap of its kin and sent rockets . . . right her away. She boosted the thrusters and sped upward. The rocket followed her into the air. She went higher and higher, then straightened. The rocket was still behind her.

What, does it have a tracker? she wondered. She zig-zagged to the left and right, trying to out-maneuver it. It kept up with her the whole time, gaining air on her.

She turned to the right again and the thing followed. She arced low. Same thing. She swooped back up, and as the thing followed her, she violently arced back down and sped toward the ground.

"Only going to get one shot at this," she said quietly.

She kept her thrusters angled to keep her descent on a steady trajectory. Soon the ground came into view and it was rushing up to meet her. When she was about to slam into it, she sharply arced upward. The rocket wasn't able to follow and exploded into the ground behind her as she made her way back up.

"Phew. That was a close one," she said.

She scanned below for the enemy rover and saw a bunch of green exos aiming their plasma streams at it. Soon, the thing went up.

Over her comm. she heard: "Good one, Fox."

What? Then she realized she had accidentally left her comm. on. Her heart rose with relief at hearing a familiar name. Which of the green exos was Nick? If it was Nick and not someone else who shared his surname. Should she try and communicate with him? What should she say?

She arced down and headed to where Riley said he was going to be. As she descended, she sent plasma bursts into any enemy exo she saw. She landed by a bunch of green ones and stood there. A moment later, a green exo came up to her.

"Riley?" she said.

"It's me."

"I heard them say 'Fox.'"

23

IT WAS A relief, Riley had to admit. Though he didn't know Nick Fox all that well—if it was him—the fact that someone here who had been part of their team prior to coming through the wall was present sent a flush of relief through him. The problem was, this *wasn't* the Nick Fox he knew, but a previous incarnation on the timeline.

"We need to talk to him," Riley said.

"And say what? That we were on the same team in the future and we've come to the past and, hello, we need your help? What help could he possibly provide anyway?"

He exhaled slowly. "I've been doing some thinking. We established when we are, but getting back—I really think that's something we can't pull off on our own. We're going to need to let someone else in on it."

"And Fox is your choice?"

"He's got the experience. Not in this specifically, but in combat and military planning. He's got some major years on us in that regard. Maybe he's got an angle we haven't considered yet?"

"What angle? Time travel—it was thought impossible until earlier today. It hasn't happened before."

"So far as you know." The words came out without him thinking about it, but he realized he had a point. What if the time portal today *wasn't* the first one? What if Manta Six had figured it out before—or at least the theory of it, conducted a few experiments, even succeeded—then realized they needed the particle accelerator to make the portal bigger? What if Riley's own side had figured it out—hence why they had the particle accelerator to begin with—but kept things dismantled for fear of misuse? Perhaps Commander Tiel hadn't told him everything. So many possibilities.

"What are you saying?"

"Not a hundred percent sure, but for something of this magnitude, I think our experience is only part of what happened, or what was planned to happen, or something."

"That's a lot of 'ors.'"

"Cut me a break, Sophie. I don't know. My head's spinning just thinking about it." He didn't mean to bark. He just wanted things to slow down, a chance to take a breather.

"So what about Fox?" Her words were stern.

"Let's find him, verify it's Nick, and see what he thinks."

"Fine. I just don't know what you're going to say."

"Me neither. We'll find out when we get there. Just . . . first things first."

He led her on through the battlefield, weaving around friendly exos. The ground was ablaze in places, chunks of dirt blown out of others. He supposed he could send out a radio message and just ask for Nick Fox, but enjoyed keeping his distance at the moment. Nick was higher up on the command chain so odds were he wouldn't just be roaming about. Now that the battle was over, protocol indicated a meet-up.

"Look for where a bunch are gathered," Riley said.

"Okay."

They made their way across the road. Up ahead, a couple green exos bounded toward a gathering of a few others, which were around the surviving enemy rover.

"There," Riley said.

They went over to it, Riley's heart pounding all the while. What was he going to say when he found Fox?

He counted off eight exos gathered in a semicircle by the rover. Perhaps Nick was on the other side, giving the next stage of the plan.

Upon closer inspection, he noted the exos were all on the defensive. Just past them, backed up against the rover, was a black exo, fully armed. It had its canon raised, pointed at the group.

A voice came over the black exo's speaker. "Stay back!"

Riley looked closely and saw its other arm aiming the attached plasma rifle right where the rover's fuel tank was. Just beyond, he saw movement inside the rover's cockpit.

It's a standoff, Riley thought. *He blows that, he blows up whoever's inside, one of his own.*

"Put the weapon down!" one of the green exos shouted.

"Not on your life!"

"There's no way out of this. You're outnumbered eight to one."

Make that ten to one, Riley thought now that he and Sophie were here.

All of the surrounding exos had their cannons pointed at the black one.

"This weapon is locked on," the black exo said. "You rush me and I take out this block." He was right. The explosion would not only take out the ten exos surrounding him, but the men inside and anyone within a thirty-meter radius.

"Get out of the suit!" Riley recognized the voice as belonging to Nick. "I mean it. Stand down."

"No! You let me out of here," the black exo said.

"I'm afraid we can't do that."

"What do we do, Riley?" Sophie asked.

He didn't respond, but instead examined the black exo-suit. It was different than some of the others he had fought during the battle. He recognized it as akin to the ones in the hangar before the wall of light opened. Was this guy from the future, had made his way—along with who knew how many others—this far out? If the game plan had been to fan out after the assault in the city, that would make sense.

The black exo was backed right up against the rover. "I'm flying out of here. No one follow."

"You're not leaving," Nick said.

"Yes, I am." He raised his cannon higher and sent out a rush of flame. The stream of it was sent along the line of the semicircle, causing everybody to move back a step. He brought the flame back around, forcing everybody back again.

Riley turned to move. "I need you to fire on him on my mark."

"Are you crazy? He'll cut loose into the rover and will send us all up in flames!"

"Do you trust me?"

It took a few seconds for her to respond. "I guess."

"'I guess' isn't good enough. I need you with me on this, Sophie."

"Then tell me what you're going to do."

He did.

"That's a long shot," she said.

"It's the only way or we're going to be standing out here all night until the guy fully panics and does indeed kill everyone."

"I'm serious," the guy in the black exo-suit said, "I'm taking off in ten seconds. You start following and this thing goes up. Ten—"

Riley slowly backed away, moving toward the left with each step.

"Nine. Eight."

He spoke to Sophie on the comm. "On three."

"*Your* three," she said, "or when he gets to three."

"When—"

The guy shouting "Seven" and "Six" drowned him out.

"What?" she said.

"Five. Four."

Riley kept moving to the side so now he was adjacent to the black exo on the other side of the green ones.

"Three—"

Sophie flew up so she could get a clear shot above the green exos and fired right at the black exo's plasma weapon. His arm swung back and hit the rover from the impact.

"You're all dead!" He shouted and opened fire on the fuel tank. Riley didn't have long before the continuous plasma blast would breach the layer of armor.

He rose up and flew in from the side, crashing into the black exo. The black exo immediately threw on its thrusters and arced up into the sky. Riley went after him. The guy shot at him from his cannon. Riley veered away from the attack and continued flying up past him. He then arced sharply in the air and landed on top of the black exo, killing his thrusters just before impact. His heavy feet crashed into the exo's shoulders, knocking it down toward the earth. Riley threw on his thrusters and opened fire with his own cannon and sent a barrage of plasma bursts at it. He then switched to the half-dozen and sent two of those his way. They hit the target dead on. Riley flew toward him and slammed into him. Metal crunched on metal and the two sped toward the earth. Just before impact, Riley adjusted his flight path, went back up a few feet, then shot the exo again, the force of the blast smashing it into the ground. He landed on top of it and wailed on him with his cannon.

He kept striking him, over and over, the heavy battering-ram of his cannon denting and crushing the metal of the black exo's head unit. Soon, the black exo-suit just lay there in a heap. Whether the guy inside was alive or not, he didn't know.

Green exos rushed over to him, some flying, others by ground.

One came up to him. "At ease, soldier. It's over." The voice seemed to belong to Nick. It was hard to tell through the speaker.

Riley got off the black exo. Heart racing, frustration from the day dumping adrenaline into his system, he wanted to keep going. He'd had enough of these stupid—

"I'll take it from here," Nick said.

"Get the suit open," Riley said.

"What's your name, soldier?"

"Riley. Riley Connor." He spoke without thinking. *Should've kept my mouth shut. Now he'll put me on his report when there's two of me here in the past. I'll be in two places at once.* He thought about lying and giving another name, but that wouldn't make any sense. He wasn't thinking straight. There was only one way out of this now. "I need to talk to you, Nick. Upper level security. And you can't go to Commander Tiel. At least, not yet."

"Commander Tiel isn't in charge of this operation. You should know that if you were one of my own. Who are you really?" Nick raised his cannon at him.

"You won't need that, I promise. I just need you to trust me."

"Hard to trust a man I can't see."

Another green exo ran up to him. The way it suddenly stopped short indicated it was Sophie inside the suit. It turned away.

"You're right," Riley said. He pressed a few buttons inside the suit and the head unit flipped up. He pressed another button and the chest piece opened. He pressed one more and the hips and legs opened up. He climbed out of the suit, hands in the air. "How 'bout now?"

24

THEY RODE IN the back of a RYN carrying unit. Riley had asked that him, Nick and Sophie ride alone, but Nick wouldn't grant the request. So they sat there in silence. Riley and Sophie were out of their suits, the suits being transported with them. Nick was still in his, as were a few other men.

"You're acting awfully strange, soldier," Nick said. "And from the looks of you, it looks like you've seen some action today."

You don't know the half of it, Riley thought. "You'll have my full cooperation once we get back to base." He couldn't believe he said the words. Back to base? Now they were in thick.

"Who's your friend?" Nick asked, nodding to Sophie. "You guys seem to be with us, looking at what you're wearing." He meant their standard-issue pants. "Unless you stole that off some of my men."

"We didn't steal it," Sophie said. "We just need you to trust us."

"I'll remind you," Riley said, "I caught that guy trying to escape then voluntarily stepped out of my suit. I even let you handcuff me." He raised his hands, showing the cuffs. Sophie was bound, too.

"Unless you planned on being caught," Nick said.

"I wasn't caught," Riley said. "I gave myself up on my own." His eyes didn't leave Nick's.

The ride back to base was going to be a long one.

STAKE 47

Riley and Sophie were led down a long corridor. Riley recognized the base as Stake 47. He remembered it from the war. Used to walk its halls before it was decommissioned. He knew they were being taken in for interrogation. He didn't think it was merited, but it just went to show how thorough Nick Fox was. He had people to answer to as well, and, Riley had to admit, his own behavior had been strange.

As he walked the passages, he looked at the other officers and thought to himself how strange an idea it was that here they were, a man and woman from the future, walking in their midst. If they only knew.

If Nick only knew and, he feared, the time to tell him was going to be sooner rather than later.

He tried his best to come up with a good way to say what needed to be said, but each mental pass at it only led to more questions, like how Nick would react. Would he even believe them? Riley was still processing the time travel himself and *he* had been the one to do the traveling. What would Nick do with the information? Submit it to Command? What would they do about it? Never mind the man in the black exo-suit they just captured. What if he talked? And where was he, anyway?

By the time they reached the interrogation room, Riley decided to simply keep the facts ordered in his mind and then address each question as they came, reveal certain items when necessary, only speak when spoken to. He hoped he could fulfill that last part because he had a tendency to speak his mind, especially when under pressure.

He and Sophie were separated. He looked at her as she was escorted out of the room, hoping to convey by his gaze both for her to trust him and for her not to offer up too much information. The last thing they needed was for them both to be locked away for reason of insanity.

Nick closed the door. A soldier stood guard beside it, still in the room. Great. Riley had hoped they would be alone.

"Have a seat," Nick said and gestured to the chair on the other side of the table.

Riley sat down. Across from him was another chair—for Nick—and beyond that a two-way mirror. There was no telling who was on the other side of it.

Nick used his pass card and unlocked the security box by the door and left the room for a moment. Riley knew that if the layout of this interrogation room was like the others on base he'd seen, then Nick had made a sharp turn to the left and entered the room behind the mirror. A moment later Nick re-emerged, a data pad in hand.

"Leave us," he told the soldier guarding the door.

"Yes, sir," the soldier said and exited.

"Okay," Nick said, "now it's just you and me." He sat down across from Riley.

"Not really," Riley said. "Who's on the other side of the mirror?" So much for only speaking when spoken to. He knew he couldn't keep that side of it.

"None of your concern."

Well, it's going to be depending on what we end up talking about, Riley thought. "Why did you take me in?" *There I go again.*

"I'll ask the questions, please."

"Fine."

Nick eyed his data pad for a few minutes then laid it flat on the table and slid it over to Riley. "Put your finger on the square."

Riley saw the data program that was running. It was for fingerprint ID. It'd scan his index finger or thumbprint and pull up his military file. "If I do that, it's going to open a door."

"Really? What kind of door?"

"Ever hear the story *Alice's Adventures in Wonderland?*"

"Not for ages, but I'm familiar with it."

"Remember the rabbit hole?"

"What are you saying?" Nick leaned forward on the desk. "See, this is why we've brought you in. Your words are threatening. You're suggesting you know something we don't and whether on our side or the enemy's, you're coming across like you've got the upper hand."

"Believe me, I don't have the upper hand. If anything, I'm at a severe disadvantage."

"How so?"

"Aside from me sitting here, being questioned as if I'm some kind of criminal instead of one of your own? I guess I'm one of those wrong-place-at-the-wrong-time types."

"So you are one of us, or, at least, want me to believe that. Put your finger on the square, please."

Riley inhaled slowly and exhaled even slower. He knew where this was headed and he didn't want just anybody knowing about it. "I'll make you a deal."

"You're not in a position to request that."

"This is what I'm offering: information that will change the course of this war for you. For me. In exchange, I want audience with you, Commander Tiel and Grayson Wilder. And the woman you brought in with me? I want her present as well. No one else. No one on the other side of the mirror. You do that, you'll have my full cooperation."

Nick pulled the data pad back toward himself and tapped the screen several times. He was probably crosschecking Grayson's name with the service files.

"And if I don't comply?" Nick asked.

"Then you and I are going to have a very long staring contest."

25

AFTER HAVING STARED at each for several minutes, Nick finally gave in. Riley presumed the man realized he wouldn't say any more unless his request was granted. Further, by bringing in the requested personnel, observation by the other soldiers would've still taken place.

They were all crammed into the interrogation room, with Riley and Sophie, still cuffed and patted down yet again, sitting on one side of the table, Commander Tiel sitting on the other. Nick and Grayson stood beside their superior. Nick's hand was on his weapon.

Tiel took a puff on his cigar. "You have to admit we've been very generous in going along with your request."

"I have but one more," Riley said.

"Oh?"

"The mics in the room. Please turn them off."

"I assure you, there's no one in the observation room."

"I'll be honest, I don't trust that. I know you like to be thorough and on top of things."

"True," Tiel said. He nodded to Grayson, who left the room. When she came back, she gave a nod in his direction.

Riley guessed that the reason Tiel and the others were being so cooperative was because, ultimately, they were in control. Him and Sophie were in a military facility, cuffed, and were inches away from Nick's weapon. They couldn't escape if they wanted to, and any trouble they would attempt to cause would be met with force.

Nick laid down the data pad, the screen again tuned in to the identifier program.

"Please press down your finger," Nick said.

Riley reached forward and put his thumb in the middle of the square. Sophie gave him a look that said, "I hope you know what you're doing."

He gave her a wink. Her return gaze said that wasn't very reassuring.

A moment later, Riley's service record came up. "As you can see," he said, "I'm one of you. But as you can also see, I'm assigned to elsewhere in this station. I wasn't even supposed to be at the battle earlier."

"We'll talk about that in a minute," Nick said. "Leaving your post and joining another mission without permission is strictly prohibited."

"It'll make sense in a moment," Riley said.

"It better," Tiel said, his voice firm.

They IDed Sophie and saw that she, too, was assigned elsewhere. Had the circumstance been different, they would've found themselves under prompt disciplinary action.

"Explain yourselves," Tiel said.

Grayson crossed her arms. Nick raised his eyebrows. It seemed his patience with all this was quickly running out.

"These records are correct in terms of where we're supposed to be," Riley said. "But they are incorrect in terms of who we are."

"Partly correct," Sophie said.

"You better start making sense," Tiel said. "I'm running out of patience."

"Then I'll tell you plainly: Sophie and I are from the future."

Tiel's eyes went wide and not from disbelief. It was clearly no surprise that Riley would try to say something like that. "Uh huh."

"It's the truth," Sophie said. "We were on assignment from you, Commander, and followed Manta Six agents to a hidden location in the hills just outside the city. We were captured and when we tried to escape, we were accidentally pulled through a vortex that brought us to the past."

"This is ridiculous," Nick said. He looked Riley in the eye. "You promised me full cooperation if I granted your request and now you're acting like children."

"I can prove it," Riley said.

"Oh yeah, how?" Grayson said. "And why did you want the five of us gathered? I don't even know them." To Tiel: "Sorry, sir. I know of you, but I've never been under your command. I'm still in training."

"It's all right, soldier," he said.

"Riley had asked for us to meet because it was this group that was formed to track down an item of importance, an item" —Sophie looked off to the side, as if putting a few puzzle pieces together— "that could be on base here right now." Then, as if in afterthought and said much quieter, "Unless it was moved here."

"And what item is that?" Nick asked.

Tiel took a puff on his cigar and tapped the end of it, dropping the ash into the ashtray.

Riley looked Tiel in the eye. "A particle accelerator."

Tiel squinted. Obviously he knew of it, even now, back here in the past. How Riley knew of it, that was no doubt the question on his mind.

"If the knowledge of that isn't proof enough," Sophie said, "then—"

Riley cut her off. "Don't say it. You know how many problems that could cause?"

"It's the only way," she said to him through gritted teeth.

"I know, but—"

"Enough," Tiel said. "Now you've really made me mad. And you know why, too." Riley knew he was referring to knowing about the particle accelerator. "You both are suspended until further notice."

Sophie shot up from her chair and slammed her hands down on the table. "You don't believe us!"

Nick pulled out his stunner. "Watch it. Sit. Down."

"It's okay, Sophie," Riley told her. "Do as he says. We have no choice but to prove it to them."

"Enlighten me because you're about to be thrown out of here," Tiel said.

Riley sighed. "Here's what I suggest you do. You—"

"You're not giving me orders."

"I'm simply making a suggestion so that you believe us and then we can move on and come up with a plan from there. Put Sophie and I in the brig. Have Grayson stand guard. In the meantime, you and Nick locate me and Sophie in our current positions. You'll see that we can't possibly be in two places at once, yet that is what you'll find. If there's two of us, then that means we've told you the truth. You can even radio into Grayson while she's watching us to confirm we didn't somehow escape and tried to pull a ruse on you. Fair?"

"I'm not going to indulge in this fantasy," Nick said. "This is ridiculous."

Tiel eyed Riley intently. Riley looked him in the eye in return.

"Do it," Tiel said. "Take them to the brig. Locate these so-called other versions of themselves."

"Please do it discreetly," Riley said. "The other her and I can't know what's going on."

"It can disrupt the timeline and make things even more complicated," Sophie said.

"We'll see," Tiel said.

"Then it's settled," Riley said. "Lock us up."

26

Sophie sat on the lower bunk while Riley laid on the floor, his knees up.

"I hate cells," Sophie said. "Especially the last one we were in."

"You're telling me," Riley said.

His eyes were closed. Sophie knew he was tired. So was she. It was tempting to just stretch out on the bunk and close her eyes, too, but she knew her anxious heart would keep her awake. Grayson stood just outside the cell door, checking in on them through the slot in the doorway, as if making sure they weren't trying to escape.

All they could do was wait while Nick and Commander Tiel tracked down the other versions of themselves and saw their duplicates. She only hoped they wouldn't say anything to them or, if they did, it would be nothing to do with what was going on.

She sighed and rubbed her eyes. Then she let out a yawn. This was going to take a while.

Time passed. She must've nodded off because the bang on the door jolted her. It was Tiel. He stood just inside the doorway. Grayson was still stationed outside it. Tiel's hands were in his pockets.

His face said it all: they found them.

"I'm seeing it, but I don't believe it," Tiel said.

Riley sat up. He must've fallen asleep, too, because he rubbed his eyes. "We were telling the truth. Did you say anything to them?"

Tiel shook his head. "No. Simply spotted them from afar and checked in with Wilder while you two were sleeping. She saw you, we saw . . . you . . . too."

"Now what?" Sophie said.

"We need to get back," Riley said.

"We need to talk," Tiel said.

"We can," Riley said, "but I don't know how much good it'll do unless you open up to us."

"And you guys open up to me." Was Tiel just offering not to be so secretive? That was a first. "I—" He was cut off when his radio chirped on.

A voice came over it, saying, "Commander, we need you. Lots of activity in the city. Yates reported the sudden emergence of enemy lines. Something about a bright blue light."

Sophie's heart sped up. "That's it! That's how we got here. Through that wall of blue light."

Tiel raised a finger to shush her. "I'll be on my way in a moment. Start mobilizing a set of three teams."

"Might need more than that, sir. Apparently enemy numbers are growing."

"I'll be right there," Tiel said.

Sophie stood. So did Riley. "We're going with you," she said.

"You're staying here. You just confirmed the existence of . . . time travel. There's much that we need to go over."

"We can't. That bright blue light might be our only way back home."

"She's right," Riley said. "If you don't let us go, her and I might be stuck here."

"If the enemy has time travel technology, I need to know how it works," Tiel said. "You need to stay here. If they have that kind of power, I need to find out what I can about it."

"You can't do this," Riley said. "Please."

"I'm sorry, but you're staying here."

Grimacing, Riley took a swing at him. Tiel took it on the jaw and stumbled over to the side. Just then a burst of electricity shot forth from the doorway. It struck Riley in the chest and sent him down. Grayson stood just beyond the door, weapon drawn.

Tiel straightened himself and pointed a finger at Sophie. "You're both on lock down." To Grayson: "See they don't leave this cell!"

"Yes, sir," she said.

Commander Tiel stormed out. Grayson closed the door.

Sophie got down beside Riley and gave him a nudge. He was out cold. "Way to go, Riley. Way to go."

◆ ◆ ◆

When Riley finally came around, Sophie was ready to knock him back out again. He'd handled it poorly. He should've pleaded their case more. *She* should've pleaded their case more as well. Instead, Riley lashed out and got himself stunned. Now here they were: stuck in a cell while Tiel was sending out troops to meet the enemy head on. The wall of light was present again, which meant so was their way home.

"That . . . sucks . . ." Riley said slowly.

"You deserved it, attacking a senior officer like that," she said.

She helped him sit up. Why was she being so nice to him? Because even though he acted rashly, she still found it charming, in a way; how he stood his ground even if that meant hitting someone.

"We need to get out of here and fast," he said.

"Any ideas?"

He bit his lower lip, wiggled his jaw side to side. "You could always talk to Grayson."

"She's not going to budge. Not being under a direct order like that. Besides, you just attacked Tiel. There's no way she's going to listen to us."

"You could at least try."

"Why me?"

"Remember you tried to negotiate with that guy in that house?"

"Yeah."

"Well, now's your chance to make up for it."

"I guess," she said. She stood and went to the door. She banged on it a few times. A moment later, the metal covering the small slit in the door slid open.

"What?" Grayson asked.

"You need to let us out," she said. "What's happening in the city—it could be Riley and me's only chance at getting home."

"I'm under strict orders to keep this door locked. End of story."

"Then please at least listen to me. Who knows how many lives are at stake? The entire war can be changed. You heard Commander Tiel. They found our duplicates, which means Riley and I were telling the truth about who we are. If we're telling the truth about that, then doesn't it make sense to at least hear me out?"

"Commander Tiel has a point, though. If the enemy has—and I can't believe I'm saying this—if the enemy has acquired time travel technology, then you need to give a detailed report as to how it all went down, what you saw, who you talked to, a *complete* report. Any and all info would be deemed important.”

“We don’t know how it works,” Sophie said, “other than that it does. We know one of its components, but that’s about it.”

“Then that piece of info could be deemed rather critical, don’t you think?”

“Look, Grayson, please, I’m begging you, let us out and let us try and get back home. We need to tell Commander Tiel—*our* Commander Tiel—what happened. Who knows? When we get back, the timeline could be altered and our Commander Tiel would have memory of meeting us back here in 2080. Your Commander Tiel would understand if you let us go because his future counterpart could talk to us.”

“Or you could tell him now, at this point in time. I’m sorry, but I’m not budging.” She slammed the covering of the slit in the door.

Sophie banged on the door. “Grayson!” She banged again. “Grayson!” She looked to Riley.

“At least you tried,” he said. “Thanks for doing that.”

“I hope you’re not being sarcastic,” she said as she came back over to him.

He got to his feet. “I’m not. You did your best. I think she got scared when you started talking about the two different Commander Tiels. It’s hard to get one’s head around that never mind any other potential talk about alterations to the timeline.”

“We can’t stay here,” she said. “Please tell me you have an idea.”

“Something came to me while you were talking. It’s a long shot, but it could work, especially if Grayson is jumpy.”

“What?”

He told her his idea.

"That is crazy."

"I know, but it's all we could do."

"When do you want to do it?"

"In a few minutes. We need to let a little time pass so it's plausible. Let's just hope the blue wall is still there."

"That's like hoping for the worst to happen to our troops."

"I know. But I'm also hoping for a way home."

◆ ◆ ◆

Sophie shrieked as loud as she could. She started bouncing foot to foot in hysterical panic.

The covering over the slit in the door slid open. "What is it?"

Sophie put a hand over her mouth then took it away and pointed to where Riley lay on the floor, convulsing, blood leaking out the corners of his mouth. "I was just trying to talk to him, to explain what happened. A few minutes later he started complaining his head hurt and his stomach ached. I thought it was stress but . . . but . . ."

Grayson's eyes filled the metal slit as she watched Riley twitch and shake on the floor.

"He won't stop," Sophie said. "Help us! He got injured earlier today. I thought he was fine. He did, too. You know he's been hurt. Look at the bruises. Now he's bleeding from the mouth."

Grayson opened the door to the cell and rushed in. "He's spitting blood."

"I know, I told you!" Sophie screamed. "Do something! Radio for help. Anything. Just . . . help him."

Grayson got on her radio. "This is Grayson Wilder at Brig—" Her words stopped when Sophie clubbed her on the back of her head, knocking her forward. It hadn't been enough to knock her out, so when Grayson started to scramble toward her to retaliate, Riley sat up and grabbed Grayson from behind, putting her in a sleeper. Not long after, Grayson went limp in his arms. He clicked her radio off. He stood then bent over and picked her up and put her on the lower bunk.

When he righted himself, he wiped the blood from his mouth. "You have no idea how much this hurts, biting my lip like that."

"I'd kiss it better if it wasn't so gross," she said. Was she flirting with him? Here? Now?

"Maybe when we get back," he said, "but right now we've got to get to the city and see if that wall of light is still there."

"Any ideas?"

"The main hangar. There's exo-suits there. Let's see what we can find."

"Lead the way," she said.

27

THE SKY

Shots were fired as Riley and Sophie flew from the Stake 47 hangar. The plasma beams came at them hard and fast and it took all of Riley's maneuvering capability to avoid getting hit.

He got on the comm. "Hold your fire. I repeat, hold your fire!"

"Stand down and return to base," came a male voice over his speaker.

"I can't do that," he replied. Grayson must've came to and alerted personnel to their escape just as they were suiting up.

"Stand down. I repeat stand down or we will remove you from the sky."

Riley checked his map and made sure he was pointed toward the city proper. He hoped the wall of light would still be up by the time he got there.

More plasma fire zipped past him. Sophie was flying just to his right. She veered off to the side, avoiding another hit.

"Please, officer, you have to let us go. Time is of the essence," Sophie said over the comm.

"You're leaving us no choice, then," the officer said.

Riley checked his scanner and noted a half dozen exos flying after them in pursuit. He didn't want to fire on them if he didn't have to. They were on the same team after all.

He arced high into the air, getting out of the direct line of attack. Plasma shots still came after him and one tagged him in the foot. It rocked his exo-suit and gave him a jolt inside it. He kept flying and aimed his cannon back at his attackers. He sent off a few shots, none direct, just enough to get them to adjust their flight pattern and buy him and Sophie some time.

The city came into view and soon they would be above downtown.

Sophie must've taken his shots as permission to return fire because she sent off several plasma shots of her own. One of them hit an exo dead on and sent it rocking back, disrupting its flight.

"Be careful," he told her over the comm.

"You are wanted for escape from the brig and for the theft of exo-suits," the officer said over the comm. "You leave us no choice but to remove you from the sky."

Just another minute or so, Riley thought. He hoped that when they arrived downtown, the heat of the battle would force the soldiers in pursuit to leave them alone and instead attack the enemy. He checked his scanner. They were almost there.

He fired back a couple of shots and hit another exo, then worked his comm. so that only Sophie could hear him. "Punch it. Give it all you got even if it ends up exhausting your thrusters. We need to stay far ahead of them."

"Understood," she said, and together they kicked their thrusters into high gear.

The burst of speed sent Riley firm against the interior of his suit. He descended at a sharp angle, again to make it more difficult for the pursuing exos to hit him.

They were over the city.

Off in the distance smoke billowed out from the top of one of the buildings. Another pillar of smoke came from the one beside it. He headed toward them.

Sophie flew in close beside him then they split off to the side as more plasma fire came in between them.

Using the smoke as cover, Riley took his suit down in between the buildings, hoping that he could lose the pursuing exos.

He adjusted his visor to filter out the smoke so he could see clearly. He knew it'd only be a matter of time before the pursuing exos would do the same. Again, he was banking on the battle to be enough to put an end to the pursuit for the time being.

"Where is it?" he said.

"The wall?" Sophie said.

"Yeah. Keep your eyes peeled."

They flew in between the buildings, rounding corners, flying over the lower rooftops. Below, exo soldiers battled it out in a deluge of plasma fire and bullets. Mech-bots walked the streets, some focusing their assault on the combating exos, others on each other.

From behind, plasma bursts hit Riley and knocked him into the side of a building. He crashed against the brick then slid down its face until he struck the ground below. His visor blinked out for a second before coming back on-line.

"Riley!" It was Sophie, panic in her voice.

"I'm okay, just got hit," he said.

Through the smoke, a black exo landed before him, cannon raised. Not wasting any time, he sent off a plasma burst at it then brought up his other hand and activated the attached machine gun. This particular model was made for ground combat and the bullets were armor-piercing rounds. He just hoped they were enough to puncture the black exo's armor. Riley activated the gun. The machine gun roared to life and he sprayed the approaching exo. The thing jerked and twitched when the bullets made contact. Riley followed up with another plasma burst and dropped it.

"Sophie, where are you?" he asked.

"About a hundred meters from your position," she said. "Looking for the wall, but with all this smoke it's difficult to see even with the visor set to see through it."

"Be mindful of what you're looking for. The wall might not be as big as the last one. I really don't know."

"Noted."

"If you find it, notify me immediately. I'll do the same."

"Roger."

He hoped she'd fare all right.

◆ ◆ ◆

THE CITY

Sophie searched the streets as she flew above them. Plasma fire streaked through the air as green and black exo soldiers battled it out on the concrete. A few of them were on rooftops, firing at each other. Some were locked in combat, each knocking at the other with their cannons.

A giant explosion sent a jolt through her chest. She looked for its source and saw an enemy mech-bot laying waste to a friendly tank with the weapon attached to its giant mechanical arm.

She turned and flew down a side street, getting out of its way.

A black exo took a shot at her from a nearby rooftop and sent her into a tailspin, which ended with her slamming into the rooftop across the way. The black exo flew over to her, landed, and aimed its weapon again. She fired at its cannon, her plasma burst striking it and knocking its arm back. She followed up with another shot to its chest unit and knocked it down. She jumped on top of it and slammed down on the head unit with her cannon before following up with a few shots from the blaster attached to her other wrist. The black exo lay there in a heap, smoke wafting up from its damaged circuitry.

A green one flew up on the rooftop beside her. For a moment she thought maybe it had come to help, but it ran toward her and she figured it must've been one of the ones pursuing them from the base. They locked together. Sophie grabbed the controls and ensured the combat program was running. She then kicked out with the heavy foot of her suit. Her metal foot slammed into the exo's leg, knocking it off balance. She then swiftly rounded behind it and pressed her cannon against the kill switch in the back. She fired off a shot and dropped it.

She stood over it and aimed her weapon squarely at him. "Open the suit."

The exo complied and a terrified pilot stared down the barrel of her weapon.

"I'm not going to hurt you," she said. "You need to tell your men to leave us alone. We're on your side and we're just trying to get back home."

"Someone on our side wouldn't fire on us."

"You fired first. You attacked us in the sky and you attacked me just now. We want nothing but peace and are only trying to defend ourselves. You need to leave us alone. Get on your comm. and relay that message to your men."

"And if I refuse? Besides, you stole the suits."

She was tempted to threaten him, force his hand, but instead she said, "I won't hurt you. We're on the same team. But we will defend ourselves." She kept her cannon leveled at him for a moment longer then walked away, hoping that did the trick.

Turning on her thrusters, she took off again, then checked her scanner for Riley's exo-suit.

He wasn't far away.

◆ ◆ ◆

Riley threw the black exo he had just taken out off himself. He was on his back on the city street, the ground crushed beneath him.

Just down the street a mech-bot was stomping in his direction, the giant cannon on one of its arms blasting at the enemy exos battling friendlies. At least it wouldn't fire on him when it got nearer.

He got up and ascended into the sky. He flew over the battlefield and kept an eye out for the wall. So far, he couldn't see it.

An enemy mech-bot rounded the corner. Was it his imagination or did its needle-nose cockpit seem to face in his direction? Riley turned around and started flying away from it. It sent off a spray of bullets. Some nicked his armor. He dove down in behind one of the buildings to get out of its way.

He quickly found himself in the middle of an exo battle. Three greens versus three black, each lined up and firing at each other. He flew in behind the black exos and fired, knocking them down one by one, enough for the attacking greens to come in and finish them off.

The battle was growing thicker, with more and more exos in the streets and on rooftops. Two giant mech-bots were up ahead, exchanging cannon fire. Flames ran from the surrounding buildings' windows.

Getting right to the heart of downtown, he saw two more mech-bots firing at each other. Two exos tangled in the air. Two more fought on the street just below them. An entire platoon of exos from both sides waged war on the concrete.

He came up on the corner of Portage and Main, the old main thoroughfare of the city before the new roads were built decades back. It used to be the hub of downtown. Tanks were rolling in, some from both sides. Some came to a stop and started firing. Others kept going.

And, there, in the middle, was the wall of light standing five stories tall and about the same wide.

28

"I FOUND IT, Sophie," Riley said over her comm. "I repeat, I found it."

"I'm on my way."

"Cancel that. The fighting's too thick. We need to regroup and assess."

"Copy that. Where?"

"I'm coming toward you. Just ascend and hover."

"Roger." She took off higher into the sky so she was well above the battle and the smoke and dust.

She waited. A lone black exo flew toward her. She opened fire and sent several plasma blasts toward it. They struck the black exo and he adjusted his flight path and flew away.

"That was easy," she said.

Moments later, Riley flew up beside her.

"I found the wall," he said.

"Good. Where?"

"Not far from here, at the old Portage and Main intersection. There's exos everywhere never mind mech-bots."

"Was there anything coming out of the wall?" she asked.

"Not that I could see, but I wasn't able to sit there and analyze it. I could be wrong."

"It's strange that it's in a different location now."

"Maybe they're able to adjust where it appears?"

"Maybe. We need to get to it and go through."

"I know."

"One option is to try and fly in and fly straight through it."

"It's risky. The battle is very thick. If we get fired at, it could all be over."

"That's why we'd have to simply make a bee-line for it and go in."

"It's enemy territory. There's more black there than anywhere else. We'd be nothing but target practice."

"Then what do you suggest? We can't just stay up here and wait it out."

"The thrusters won't last that long that's for sure."

"Any ideas?"

"I'll think of something."

◆ ◆ ◆

If Riley ever felt the pressure to make a decision, it was now. This was their chance. There was no telling how much longer the wall would be standing, but with the sheer amount of enemy forces nearby it didn't afford them the chance to simply walk up to it and go in. Besides, he'd taken enough damage already and wasn't sure how much longer his suit would hold out, and judging by the burn marks on Sophie's, it didn't appear hers had much juice left either.

They couldn't take the hostiles head on, and while Sophie had a point about trying to make a bee-line for the portal, he couldn't chance one of them falling along the way.

"I have an idea," he said. "It's a risk, but I think it's a safer bet than just trying to get through on our own."

"I'm all ears," she said.

When he told her his idea, her comm. was silent.

"I know, it's crazy," he said.

"We're not trained for that," she said. A pause, then, "But I like it."

Leave it to Sophie to always be up for an adventure.

They flew in toward the battle, grouped together. Their target should be right about—

Below, an enemy mech-bot was stomping its way away from its own men and blasting at the row of tanks closing in on it. Riley did a flyby and surveyed the mech-bot. It was covered in black metal shielding, the cockpit hinged between two giant legs that had joint capability around the knees. Arms were outstretched alongside the cockpit, each outfitted with a cannon, enormous Gatling guns, and most likely laser capability as well. Right now it was sending plasma bursts at the tanks.

"It's now or never," Riley said. "Stay close."

They flew in nearby the enemy mech and Riley landed on its hull. He surveyed the cockpit and found where the hatch met its body. Sophie landed, too.

They each took a side and activated the laser cutters on their suits. Immediately they got to work cutting the thing open. The mech-bot stopped its assault on the tanks. No doubt the pilots within were seeing sparks as he and Sophie cut into it.

"Get ready for them to fire as soon as it's open," he said.

They continued to work for a couple of minutes and then four black exos flew up to meet them.

Enemy backup.

Riley sent a plasma blast into one, knocking it off the cockpit. Sophie opened up her machine gun on another and fired at it. It shot a plasma beam at her. She maneuvered to the side and got out of its way before returning fire with one of her own. She knocked it off the cockpit as well.

The other two opened fire. Riley took a hit dead on and he felt the legs of his exo buckle. Sophie charged the enemy and took it down, then fired a shot into the remaining exo unit. Riley came at the same one with his cannon and struck it. With the barrel of his cannon up close, he shot it in the chest and blasted it off the cockpit. The one wrestling with Sophie righted itself while Sophie was still down. Together, he and Sophie shot it and sent it off just as another one—or the same one he had knocked off first—flew in. Riley took his laser cutter and brought the beam across the front of the unit, slicing into its armor. Sophie ran up to it from behind and shot the kill switch in the back. The thing shut down. Riley kicked it off the cockpit. Another one of the ones they had knocked off flew back on. As it flew overhead, Sophie took her laser cutter and cleaved the legs off the unit, no doubt slicing the legs off of the pilot inside in the process. The thing tumbled to the ground below.

"Nice shot," Riley said.

"Thanks," she replied.

They resumed work on opening the cockpit and were able to cut away at the canopy. Using their exos' enhanced strength, they pried at the metal and ripped the canopy off, revealing the pilots within. The pilots had handhelds and opened fire. Sophie cut one's hand off with the laser cutter, then jumped into the wide cockpit—suit and all—and swung her cannon around like a baseball bat. She knocked out both the pilots.

Riley jumped in and opened his suit. "Good going."

She powered down and stepped out of her suit as well. "All in a day's work."

They immediately took to the controls and Riley worked the weapons while Sophie drove the mech-bot. The enormous machine stomped back toward the wall of light. Riley aimed its cannon at the enemy exos below and started picking them off one by one. He could only imagine what this must look like from the ground and how the friendly forces would wonder what was going on.

He stomped on some of the exos while blasting into others as he cleared a path closer to the wall. Suddenly what sounded like cannon fire started rocking the machine. He peered out of the side of the unit and saw Expherion tanks shooting at him. They had no idea they were on his side despite what he was doing to the enemy forces.

He couldn't return fire lest he kill some of his own. Instead he pressed onward, shooting down as many Supremech exos on ground level as he could.

Another enemy mech-bot was over to the side.

"Take us up to the wall," he said.

Sophie complied and brought the mech-bot about thirty feet from it.

"Maneuver it around so we're facing southeast."

She did. They were facing the enemy mech-bot. Riley locked on the rocket launchers and set it to fire in five minutes.

"We haven't got much time," he said.

Quickly, they suited up again. Riley double checked the controls once more and verified that a few minutes after they left the cockpit the mech-bot would fire on one of its own.

"Hurry!" he shouted above the din of battle.

They activated their thrusters and flew out of the cockpit and landed on the street below.

"Straight for it, no looking back," he told Sophie.

"Copy," she said.

They readied their weapons and bounded through the flimsy remainder of the enemy ranks. One exo came in and grabbed her. Riley cleaned it off with a plasma blast, enough for her to start running again. One came in for him, firing. It struck his unit and the controls shut down.

"Sophie!" he shouted into the comm.

No reply. His communications were out.

He couldn't see either, his visuals having gone down with the rest of the suit. He had no choice but to abandon it. Another blast rocked his suit and sent him to the ground. All he could do was lay there and hope the exo that attacked him wouldn't finish him off.

Epilogue

Sophie saw Riley's unit go down. *No looking back,* he had told her.

She briefly debated going back for him and knew she couldn't live with herself if she let him die so she stopped and doubled back and shot away the enemy exo that had its cannon aimed at Riley's fallen unit. She opened fire again, sending several more plasma bursts straight into the enemy unit for good measure.

Behind her, a rocket went off. She turned and saw the mech-bot they just abandoned fire a missile directly into its counterpart. The other mech went up in a huge explosion, its cockpit falling from between its enormous mechanized legs.

Back to Riley.

She turned and saw him climbing out of his suit.

"Come on!" she shouted over the speaker. She led the way to the wall and was soon encompassed by blue light.

◆ ◆ ◆

INSIDE THE WALL

Riley's skin alit with fiery electricity the moment he entered the wall. It crackled around him as he ran forward, the sound of plasma and machine gun fire growing more and more distant behind him.

Then there was silence aside from the crackling of the electricity.

Shortly after, he emerged in the hangar in the hills again. The room was near empty, a few straggling troops finishing entering the wall as he ran off to the side. Where was Sophie?

Weapons fire broke out and he wondered what was going on. Soon green exos filled the room and he was relieved to see friendly weaponry.

He looked over to the portal generator. A few scientists worked the controls while some of the others around them raised their hands in surrender. He spotted Sophie and ran toward her.

She climbed out of her suit to greet him. He couldn't help but hug her.

"We made it!" he said.

She squeezed him tight. "I know. It's awesome. We're back."

He held her a moment then a green exo came up to them.

"There you are." Riley recognized the voice as belonging to Nick—his Nick. "I suggest you stand back." His exo-suit was facing the wall.

"Don't go in there," Riley said.

"Noted."

Another exo came up alongside Nick. "You found them." It was no doubt Grayson. "What's—what's going on?"

"Don't go near it," Sophie said.

Riley looked at the scientists by the controls. His fellow officers were beginning to round them up.

He looked back to Nick. "How long were we gone?" Riley asked.

"A week. We were sent in to find you," Nick said. "We came in today and have been clearing this place out."

Riley shook his head. "I meant . . . . Never mind. I'll fill you in later."

Nick turned to Sophie. "Where did you get that suit?"

One of the scientists broke free and warned everyone to stay away. Nick raised his weapon. "Drop it!"

The scientist held his gun aloft and brought it to his head. He also produced a controller from his pocket. "Manta Six. This war is ours." He pressed the button on the control and giant metal doors opened up behind the wall of blue light.

Riley's jaw dropped. He had thought it was just an ordinary wall, but instead on the other side of it was a legion of black exo soldiers and an armada of enemy mech-bots. He could tell Nick was at a loss for words. So was Grayson.

"Riley . . ." Sophie said.

The fleet of black exos started marching toward the blue wall, entering it from the other side. Soon the mech-bots behind them began to mobilize.

Riley was jolted from the scene when the scientist shot himself.

"The first time was just a test . . ." Riley said. "This had been their plan all along."

Green exos got into action and began attacking the front lines of the black ones trying to enter the wall. Plasma fire was exchanged and the greens were quickly overrun.

"They're going to change history," Sophie said. "There's so many of them."

Riley understood. The battle they'd just come from was simply to draw out Expherion troops, get most of them in one place. Now they would send in all they had and completely overcome them.

"I can't let this happen," Riley said.

Not knowing how long the portal would remain open, he started running toward the wall. Sophie bolted after him. "Where are you going?"

"To warn them," he shouted over his shoulder. He picked up his speed and kept his eyes ahead.

"No!" she screamed.

Riley put her cries behind himself, entered the wall, and was surrounded by blue light.

Continued in

Mech Apocalypse 2

About the Author

A.P. Fuchs is the author of many novels and short stories. His most recent books are *Axiom-man: Outlaw; Axiom-man: Episode No. 2: Underground Crusade; Getting Down and Digital: How to Self-publish Your Book; Look, Up on the Screen! The Big Book of Superhero Movie Reviews; Canadian Scribbler: Collected Letters of an Underground Writer*, and *Redemption of the Dead*, the third book in his time travel zombie trilogy.

Also a cartoonist, he is known for his superhero series, *The Axiom-man Saga*, both in novel and comic book format.

Fuchs's main website is **www.canisterx.com**

You can also sign up for Fuchs's free weekly newsletter, *The Canister X Transmission*, at **www.tinyletter.com/apfuchs**

www.ingramcontent.com/pod-product-compliance
Lightning Source LLC
Chambersburg PA
CBHW061436210726
48287CB00007B/2245